Rui and the Pen

DAVID LAWRENCE

ILLUSTRATED BY CHERIE DIGNAM

EK

First published 2023

EK Books
an imprint of Exisle Publishing Pty Ltd
PO Box 864, Chatswood, NSW 2057, Australia
226 High Street, Dunedin, 9016, New Zealand

A CiP record for this book is available from the National
Library of Australia.

ISBN 978-1-922539-38-0

Designed by Mark Thacker
Typeset in Minion Pro 12 on 18pt
Printed in China

This book uses paper sourced under ISO 14001 guidelines
from well-managed forests and other controlled sources.

10 9 8 7 6 5 4 3 2 1

To all those who wish they had a magic
pen to sort out their problems.

CHAPTER

1

Ruby stopped doodling and sat perfectly still on her bed.

An argument had started in the next room, and she strained her ears to listen to the slightly muffled words.

'… but she doesn't say *anything*. She just sits there and draws. It's creepy!'

The angry voice belonged to her mother's latest boyfriend, David Sykes.

Ruby glanced down at the cartoon drawing of him that she was working on. It greatly accentuated his beady eyes, sweaty brow and comical comb-over hairstyle.

Mmmm, maybe I've been too kind, she thought. She added the words 'Dodgy Dave' to the top of the drawing, as her mum's weary voice carried through the wall.

'Come on, it hasn't been easy for Ruby …'

'Easy for Ruby? What about *me*, Adelaide?' roared Dodgy Dave.

Ruby rolled her eyes and crossed her arms as the indignant rant continued.

'Do you have any idea how much it's going to cost me to send her to boarding school?'

Ruby knew the exact amount — because Dodgy Dave reminded her every day.

'*And* I had to call in a huge favour from the headmaster to get *your* daughter to the top of the waiting list.'

'And I … *we* appreciate that,' said Adelaide.

'Do you *really*?'

'Yes, of course we do!'

Dodgy Dave's voice softened.

'Hey, at least when she's gone it'll give us some time together. You know, just the two of us …'

Ruby put her fingers in her mouth and pretended to vomit.

She jumped off the bed to take a closer look at a vibrant seascape painting hanging on the wall. Powerful foaming waves crashed over sleek dark rocks, and a brilliant bolt of lightning fractured the stormy grey sky.

As always, her eyes were drawn to the artist's signature in the bottom right-hand corner:

B.A. West.

Ruby looked back at the candle sitting on her bedside table, then wandered over and picked up the well-worn leaflet next to it. On the front cover it said, 'In loving memory of Bertie Arthur West.' Ruby turned to the back page where there were some photos of her father, and tears instantly formed in her eyes.

They were mainly family snaps, and Bertie's radiant smile was prominent in all of them. He had a shock of thick dark hair, a kind face and a very questionable taste in fashion. When asked about his tendency to wear loose-fitting Hawaiian shirts and tracksuit pants, he'd always say, 'I'm just going to get covered in paint, so I may as well be comfortable.'

Ruby looked at the photos again, this time focusing on her mum. Shoulder length, sandy blonde hair, a cute button noise and piercing blue eyes — she looked stunning. Adelaide was still attractive, but to Ruby she no longer resembled the dazzling woman in the photos next to her father. Ruby tried to think of the most accurate words to describe her mother at the moment, and the first ones to pop into her head were 'lost', 'broken' and 'a complete mess'.

Ruby's eyes moved to her own image in a photo taken just before Bertie's death. She was sitting on her dad's shoulders with a grin from ear to ear, and they both had multi-coloured flecks of paint on their faces. Back then she was eight years old, contented and carefree.

She put down the leaflet, then went over to stare into the mirror above her desk. Her unkempt, mousy coloured hair hung down so that it partially obscured her large brown eyes. Those eyes that sparkled in the photos now appeared much darker, as if their light had been snuffed out. Her face was damp and puffy from crying, and there was an accidental red marker blotch on her cheek that resembled a pimple.

'Lookin' good Rubes,' she whispered.

It was exactly four years ago that Bertie had died, and this morning she had lit the candle to honour his life. Unfortunately, the flame had set off a smoke alarm, and Dodgy Dave had gone ballistic.

She had been 'grounded' in her room ever since.

Walking back to her bed, Ruby tripped over an open suit-case in the middle of the floor. Her half-packed bags were a reminder of how little time remained before she had to leave for boarding school. A sudden surge of resentment towards her mother rose from the pit of her stomach.

Thanks Mum. Another boyfriend. Another school.

Only this time the new school was in another state.

Ruby angrily tossed the 'Dodgy Dave' drawing under the bed, on top of the ones of her mum's previous boyfriends.

They also had titles: 'Caveman Carlos', 'Lazy Luke', 'Toupee Ted' and 'Bad Breath Barry'.

She picked up a roll of sticky tape, ripped off a small strip, then positioned it so that half was stuck to the bedroom door and the other half to the frame. This was a trick her dad had taught her, to detect if anyone entered her room while she wasn't there. He'd called it, 'The world's cheapest security alarm'.

After pulling on a dark blue hoodie, Ruby picked up her sketch pad and crept over to the window. She gently released the lock, quietly pushed up the frame, and silently slipped outside. Ruby scaled the streaky grey wooden fence at the back of the house, then walked briskly up a narrow laneway that led to the corner of a main road. She looked back to make sure no one had seen her — not that she really cared about being caught. The worst thing they could do was send her to boarding school, and they were already doing that.

Ruby set out for the mall, keeping her head down to avoid eye contact with passers-by. She picked up an abandoned green milk crate that was lying on the footpath and found a spot out the front of a very small bookstore called Book World. *Wow, if this is Book World, Book City must be tiny!*

She sat down on the crate, pulled

Dodgy Dave

8

out a black marker and scribbled a sign that said, 'Cartoon drawings, ten dollars!'

An hour passed without any customers, and Ruby was about to give up when a young couple slowed down as they were walking by.

'Hey, can you do a funny drawing of my boy-friend?' asked the woman with a cheeky grin.

'No way!' said her boyfriend.

'Yes way! And draw something to do with his mum. He's *really* scared of her and does everything she says.'

'I do not!'

'Really? She calls you up to water her garden, and you go around straight away.'

'What's wrong with that?'

'Um, right in the middle of my birthday lunch …'

While the couple bickered, Ruby drew a cartoonish pic-ture of the boyfriend in an army helmet saluting a scary old-er woman in a uniform, covered with medals.

At the bottom she added the words: 'Yes sir, Mummy sir!'

She held up the drawing and the girlfriend burst out laughing.

Caveman Carlos

'That is brilliant!' she said. 'Pay the girl.'

'I'm not paying for that!'

'Why not?'

'What if my mum sees it?'

'Oh, you are *pathetic*!' said the girlfriend, reaching into her handbag.

She scrounged around for a while before looking at Ruby apologetically.

'I've only got, um … five dollars and … twenty-five cents, sorry.'

Ruby gratefully stuffed the money into her pocket, and watched the young couple continue to argue as they strode off.

'You cannot show that to my mother!'

'Show her? I'm framing it and giving it to her for Christmas …'

As Ruby weighed up what to do next, she spotted a billboard advertising the local Sunday market.

With a shrug of her shoulders, she ambled off in that direction.

As she started walking, the temperature suddenly dropped dramatically, and a small shiver went down her spine. Behind her a thick fog began rolling slowly down the mall, swallowing traffic lights, cars, buildings and everything else in its path. This spectacular blanket of mist seemed to follow Ruby to the market, where she was greeted by a wonderful variety of sounds and smells.

The aroma of sausages and onions blended nicely with the gentle wafts of Indian curries and Spanish seafood paella. Peals of laughter rang out through the foggy haze, as well as the voices of stall vendors offering their wares, and enthusiastic bargain hunters gently haggling over prices.

After half an hour of aimlessly wandering around, a stall suddenly appeared in front of Ruby. This was strange because she had already been along this particular row twice without noticing it. *Must have missed it in the mist,* she thought.

It was a quirky-looking stall with a worn plastic banner that said, 'Second Hand Treasures'. Ruby glanced down at the rickety wooden trestle table that was covered with a variety of items, including antique clocks, painted plates and colourful figurines. She was about to move on when a flash of gold from the far end of the table caught her attention.

It was a pen.

A very old-looking pen.

She moved closer to take a better look. It was a deep wooden brown, but its exterior was so scratched and worn, it looked like it had been placed in a tumble dryer for a week.

Ruby tentatively picked it up, and without any warning

a surge of warm energy flowed through her fingertips, then spread throughout her entire body. All her problems seemed to disappear, and it felt like she was wearing an invisible suit of armour.

'Nothing can harm me,' she whispered.

As she studied the pen in more detail, she discovered there were some strange words inscribed in gold on its side. *'Manibus futuri.'*

'You like it?' came a deep voice from the other side of the trestle table. It belonged to a peculiar-looking, grey-haired old man. He had a weathered, leathery face and mischievous eyes, and he wore a purple robe covered in gold coloured images of moons and stars, with a matching brimless cap.

'So, you like it?' repeated the man.

'Um, yeah, it's cool.'

Ruby inspected the pen again.

'Can you tell me what, um, Man-i-bus fu-tu-ri means?'

'It's Latin and it means, "The future is in your hands".'

'I wish,' muttered Ruby.

She wanted this pen more than anything in the world, and slowly looked up and asked, 'Um, h-how much?'

The old man paused to study her. His eyes narrowed and he folded his arms as if he was weighing up an important decision. He reminded Ruby of a judge on a TV talent show.

He suddenly unfolded his arms and said, 'Five dollars and twenty-five cents.'

Ruby's spirits soared and she hurriedly pulled out all the money from her pocket and placed it on the table.

'Five dollars and twenty-five cents exactly!'

With her heart pounding, Ruby picked up her new, very old pen, and quickly turned to walk away. She was desperate to escape before the man changed his mind.

'Hey wait!'

Ruby froze.

With a sinking feeling in her stomach, she slowly turned around.

'Don't forget the ink,' said the man with a smile.

He carefully handed Ruby a small square bottle filled with a dark blue liquid.

She nodded, slid the bottle into her hoodie pocket and hastily set off.

After travelling about twenty metres she turned around to take one last look at the old man and his mysterious stall. However, they had both been completely enveloped by the swirling mist, giving the impression they had vanished into thin air.

CHAPTER

2

**Ruby climbed through her bedroom window, then tiptoed
to the door to inspect the strip of sticky tape.** It remained
unbroken. *Phew!*

She took the pen and the bottle of ink from her pocket
and placed them on her desk to examine them more closely. She had never used an ink pen, and had no idea what
to do next. She cautiously unscrewed the lid of the bottle,
then picked up the pen. Once again, a wonderful warm glow
spread throughout her body.

Ruby's eyes glazed over and she let out a contented sigh.
She felt like she was in a wonderful dream as she dipped the
nib into the blue pool of ink, and instinctively flicked up a
small gold lever on the side of the pen. The dark liquid started to bubble as it was sucked into the tip, and this reminded
Ruby of a quote from one of her dad's favourite plays.

Double, double toil and trouble,
Fire burn, and cauldron bubble.

Bertie loved to recite these words whenever he was stirring a saucepan in the kitchen. Ruby had no idea what they meant, but her dad used to say them in a cackling witch's voice, which always made her laugh.

When the bubbling stopped, she unconsciously snapped the lever back down and grabbed a sheet of paper from the top drawer. She took a deep breath and a feeling of excitement grew as she slowly lowered the pen. Just as the nib was about to touch the paper, Dodgy Dave burst into the room and Ruby spun around to face him.

'I hope you've learnt your lesson young lady!'

No, but I did sneak out and buy a really cool pen, thought Ruby.

Dodgy Dave glanced at the bags in the middle of the floor.

'You haven't finished packing!'

Ruby gripped the pen tightly in her hand and looked her mother's boyfriend directly in the eye.

'Well spotted, Sherlock Holmes!'-

Ruby's eyebrows shot upwards. Her sarcastic response was supposed to stay in her head, but had somehow tumbled out of her mouth.

Dodgy Dave was just as surprised. Ruby had never spoken back to him before — in fact, she had hardly ever spoken to him at all. His eyes bulged, his face turned bright red and he started coughing like a cat with a fur ball stuck in its throat.

'*[Cough, cough]* You *[cough, cough]* … think that's funny?'

Ruby did, but she managed to keep her thoughts to herself this time.

'Finish packing *immediately*! And after dinner, it's straight to bed as the taxi's picking you up at five-thirty in the morning.'

Ruby folded her arms and gently shook her head.

'Don't give me that look! I'll be way too busy to drive you to the airport.'

'But Mum could …'

'As if I'd let her anywhere near my Porsche,' sneered Dodgy Dave.

He stormed out as Ruby quietly screwed the cap back onto the pen and replaced the lid on the ink bottle.

'We'll have to do this some other time,' she said placing her new, treasured possession into her alligator-shaped pencil case.

The pencil case was an *old* treasured possession. It had been a seventh birthday present from Bertie, and on the accompanying card he had written, 'Here's a gift you can get your *teeth* into and give your drawings a bit more *bite*'.

It was corny, but it had made her laugh.

She turned to the bags in the middle of the room and frowned. On a whim, she theatrically pointed at her suitcase and said, 'Abracadabra!'

But the suitcase stubbornly refused to pack itself.

Ruby's alarm went off early the next morning, and she reluctantly crawled out of bed.

As she made herself breakfast, the only sound in the house was Dodgy Dave's snoring. 'Yeah, *way* too busy to take me to the airport,' she muttered.

While she was finishing off some cereal, her mum entered the kitchen and sat down at the table. Adelaide's face looked haggard, and she avoided looking Ruby in the eye.

'How are you feeling?' she asked Ruby.

'Okay,' replied Ruby quietly.

'You'll make some amazing new friends at Hetherington Hall, and going away is like a big adventure …'

Ruby felt like screaming, 'If it's *so* good, why don't you send *yourself* to boarding school?'

Instead, she took a deep breath and said, 'Sure, Mum.'

'And Dave says it's one of the best schools in the country …'

'I have to clean my teeth,' interrupted Ruby as she hurriedly stacked her cereal bowl into the dishwasher and raced out of the kitchen.

After packing her tattered toiletries bag into the suitcase, Ruby dragged her luggage into the hallway where Adelaide was waiting for her.

'You got everything?'

Ruby nodded and stared vacantly out the window. After what seemed like an eternity, Adelaide broke the awkward silence.

'Rubes … I'm really sorry … but it's probably for the best, as I'm … a bit messed up at the moment …'

'Taxi's here,' said Ruby as a yellow car pulled up in front of the house. Adelaide sighed and went to help Ruby with her bags.

'I've got it, Mum.'

Just before Ruby hopped into the cab, Adelaide rushed over and gave her a hug.

'I'll miss you, Rubes.'

There was so much Ruby wanted to say to her mum in that moment. *I love you. I hate you. I'm scared for you. I'm scared for me.* But with all those thoughts swirling around inside her head, all she managed was a quick nod, before hopping into the back of the taxi.

Ruby was determined not to look back as the taxi drove off, but she snuck a peak in the rear-view mirror and saw a tear rolling down her mother's cheek.

Ruby glanced at herself in the mirror, and noticed a tear slowly sliding down her face, too. *Twins.*

Despite the miserable start to the day, Ruby was excited about travelling on a plane for the first time.

Unfortunately, she found herself seated between two very large and inconsiderate travellers, who she nicknamed Mr and Mrs Rude. Throughout the flight she was elbowed from either side, and she suspected Mr Rude had forgotten to have a shower that morning. The smell was so bad that Ruby wished an air mask would drop from the ceiling.

The low point came when Mrs Rude fell asleep on Ruby's shoulder and drooled all over her jumper. She took the plastic-coated in-flight dining menu from the seat pocket and used it to scrape off the thick gooey liquid. *Ewwwwwww!*

But it was when Mr Rude removed his shoes and started to floss his teeth that Ruby finally decided that she *had* to escape. She politely woke up an extremely unimpressed Mrs Rude, then headed to the toilet with her sketch pad and a pencil. Once the door was safely bolted shut, she sat down and drew a cartoon about her horrible plane experience. At the bottom she added the words: 'In-flight *whini*ng'.

Like every other time Ruby finished a drawing, she wished she could show it to her father. She knew it would put a smile on his face and that thought made her happy. But it also reminded her about how much she missed him, and that made her sad.

She let out a small sigh as the flight attendant's voice came over the intercom.

'We will be landing shortly, so please return to your seats, make sure your tray tables are up, and your seats are returned to the upright position ...'

Ruby was relieved that her flying ordeal was nearly over, and after sitting next to Mr and Mrs Rude she had a brand-new perspective on life.

At least boarding school can't be <u>this</u> bad!

CHAPTER

3

As Ruby's taxi arrived at her new school, she noticed a hefty square billboard with neat blue writing attached to the tall, white picket fence.

**HETHERINGTON HALL IS AN EXCLUSIVE
CO-EDUCATIONAL SCHOOL
with two boarding houses —
one for girls and one for boys.
Brand new facilities with old-fashioned values.**

The picture on the billboard showed three happy schoolkids standing next to an awkward-looking man wearing an academic hat and gown. His cheesy grin contrasted sharply with his angry eyes.

That smile has to be photoshopped, thought Ruby.

At the very bottom was a glib slogan:

'Hetherington Hall: Producing Tomorrow's Leaders
Today!'
—Mr Oliver Lemon, Headmaster

The taxi drove through a set of intimidating dark metal gates
to reveal several large green manicured sporting ovals and a
number of impressive-looking buildings, some made of age-
ing red brick and some of warm, yellow-brown sandstone.

As the car pulled up in front of a sign marked 'School
Administration', Hetherington Hall seemed almost deserted.
The only sound Ruby could hear was a large ride-on lawn-
mower on a nearby oval, being driven by a groundsman with
the bushiest sideburns she had ever seen. She shut her eyes
and imagined drawing a cartoon of the man with birds nest-
ing comfortably on either side of his face. She even thought
of a caption: *When it's time to visit the barber!*

Ruby said goodbye to the cab driver, then lugged her suitcase and bag through a door labelled 'Reception' and walked
over to the counter. The stern-looking woman on the other
side of the glass said 'Yes?' without looking up, and kept tap-
ping away on her keyboard.

'Um, I'm looking for the girls' boarding house.'

'Sure. You turn right as soon as you leave this building, then take the next left and you'll see a long corridor.

Go down that corridor until the end, then slip through the courtyard and take a hard right, where you walk around the Raleigh-Hinds oval until you see three pathways. Take the third one that leads to a group of buildings, and *behind* those buildings are two more buildings and your boarding house is the one on the right.'

At no point did the woman make eye contact with Ruby or even slow down her typing.

'Um, okay … thanks.'

Ruby struggled out the door with her bags and hesitated. *Did she say turn left or right?*

With a shrug, Ruby turned left, and immediately crashed into a man and a woman who were coming the other way. The woman had a warm smile and stunning green eyes that sparkled like emeralds. The man was tall, athletic and had perfect dark skin. He had a welcoming grin that put Ruby at ease straight away.

'Hi,' said the woman, 'You look a bit lost — can we help?'

'I'm, um, looking for the boarding house.'

'That's where I'm heading — you must be Ruby?'

Ruby nodded nervously.

'Great! I'm Miss Atkinson, one of the teachers who lives in the boarding house … and this is Marley, I mean Mr Chol. He's another teacher, but he lives in the boys' boarding house.'

'Hey, Ruby,' said Mr Chol.

Miss Atkinson picked up Ruby's suitcase and said, 'Come on, I'll help settle you in.'

She then turned to Mr Chol and poked out her tongue.

He laughed and said, 'See you later, Faith.'

'Not if I see you first!'

'Fun-nee!' said Mr Chol.

It was a long walk to the boarding house, but Miss Atkinson was so easy to talk to that it seemed to take no time at all.

'I teach art by the way,' she said.

A smile instantly broke out on Ruby's face.

'A-ha! You're an artist!' said Miss Atkinson.

'Kind of ... I like to draw.'

'That's all I did as a kid. But it was tough because my parents made me draw right handed, even though I was left handed.'

Ruby's eyes widened in horror.

'Don't worry — they didn't know any better. Hey, are you a "lefty" or a "righty"?'

'A "righty",' said Ruby holding up her right hand to make sure there was no confusion.

'Cool ... ah, here we are,' said Miss Atkinson pointing to a large, neat two-storey red brick building with an attractive three-tiered fountain out the front. Ruby watched the water gently cascade down into a large circular pool at the base — it looked almost deep enough to swim in.

They walked inside through a red double door, and as they approached a wide set of marble stairs, a high-pitched sound stopped them in their tracks. Ruby looked to where the noise had come from and saw a fit-looking woman wearing a blue tracksuit and a whistle around her neck, rushing towards them.

The tracksuited woman had short, dyed-blonde hair and she looked Ruby up and down, before letting out a disappointed sigh.

'Ruby West, this is the boarding house mistress, Miss Luxton,' said Miss Atkinson.

'Thank you, Miss Atkinson — I'll take it from here,' said Miss Luxton.

'But—'

'No buts! Off you go. Shoo!'

Miss Luxton waited for the young teacher to leave, before bombarding Ruby with questions.

'So, which soccer team do you barrack for? What position do you play? Have you won any best and fairest awards?'

Ruby remained silent.

'Oh no, don't tell me! Have you ever played soccer before?'

Ruby shook her head.

Miss Luxton rolled her eyes. 'Unbelievable!'

Without offering to help with Ruby's luggage, the boarding house mistress blew her whistle and motioned for Ruby to follow her. She led Ruby upstairs to a spacious, white-walled dormitory that contained six immaculately made beds. Each bed had a modern desk and chair next to it, as well as a stylish brown cupboard with a set of drawers inside.

There were four girls in school uniform hanging out in the dorm, and as soon as Ruby entered they stopped talking and stared at her.

Miss Luxton pointed to the far corner and said, 'Unpack your gear then place your bags neatly under your bed. Dinner is in the dining hall at 6 p.m., don't be late! Hey Sasha, how about you help Ruby feel at home?'

'Sure, Miss Luxton,' said a tall, attractive, blonde-haired girl in a sweet voice.

All the girls had name plates on their desk, so Ruby could see that Sasha's full name was Sasha Sword. She looked at her own desk and saw the name Molly Lane, although someone had crossed out the 'n' and replaced it with an 'm' so that it said 'Molly *Lame*'.

Miss Luxton rushed over and slid the Molly Lame name plate into her tracksuit pocket.

'We'll get you your own one of these A-SAP,' she said.

The boarding house mistress then strode out of the room, and seconds later Ruby heard the shrill blast of her whistle, followed by, 'Hey — no running in the corridor!'

Ruby started unpacking her gear, but stopped when she sensed someone standing behind her. She spun around to find Sasha and another tall girl staring at her menacingly.

'Hey, newbie,' sneered Sasha. 'We need to talk.'

Ruby ignored them and went back to unpacking.

'Check out the jumper, Miranda,' said Sasha, reaching out and examining the texture of Ruby's pullover. 'I'm guessing "home-brand"!'

Miranda burst out laughing and said, 'What about the hairstyle?'

'Hairstyle?' said Sasha. 'I can see the hair, but where's the style?'

The other girls in the dorm all laughed.

Ruby turned away from her tormentors and started placing her school uniforms in the cupboard. Sasha glanced over at Ruby's open suitcase and smirked.

'Comics? What are you, like, five years old?'

Ruby continued to ignore the teasing, which caused Sasha to fold her arms and frown. She looked like a dog owner, whose disinterested Labrador was refusing to fetch a tennis ball.

Suddenly Sasha's eyes lit up. She snatched Ruby's alligator pencil case out of her bag and held it above her head.

'Check this out!' she sneered. 'She's more like a *three* year old.'

Sasha unzipped the pencil case and peered inside.

'Ooh, what's this?' said Sasha holding up the old pen.

Ruby's eyes flashed wildly.

'Give me that!'

'Oooh … she *can* talk!'

Ruby lunged to grab the pen, but the bully was too quick. Sasha lobbed it over to the raven-haired Miranda, who caught it gleefully.

'I love "Keepings off"!" she squealed.

Ruby frantically ran between the two girls as they toyed with her.

'You must *love* this pen,' said Sasha. 'But now it's time to say … goodbye!' Sasha bolted to the window and flung the pen as far as she could.

Ruby raced over and poked her head outside. There was a long, thick hedge about thirty metres away, and she realized her pen could have landed anywhere inside it.

'Wotcha gonna do now?' taunted Sasha.

Ruby turned and sped out of the dorm, to the sound of raucous laughter.

CHAPTER
4

Ruby arrived at the vast green hedge, and desperately started probing inside its dense, prickly foliage. She was familiar with the saying about 'trying to find a needle in a haystack' and decided that 'finding a pen in a giant hedge' was just as difficult.

After half an hour of frantic searching, her hands were severely scratched and her precious pen was still missing.

'What's up, Ruby?' asked a friendly voice.

She turned around and saw Miss Atkinson.

'Looking for my pen,' replied Ruby with a slight tremor in her voice.

'How did it get outside?'

'Um ...'

Miss Atkinson nodded slowly.

'Don't worry, I can probably guess. Let's go upstairs and sort this out.'

Ruby trailed the young teacher back into the dorm, and straight away all the girls fell silent.

'Sasha and Miranda, could you come over here please?' said Miss Atkinson in a calm but serious voice.

Both girls went bright red and walked over sheepishly.

'Do either of you have anything to tell me?'

'No,' said Sasha innocently.

'We don't know anything about Ruby's pen,' said Miranda.

Sasha rolled her eyes and hissed, 'You are *so* dumb!'

'I didn't mention Ruby's pen, Miranda,' said Miss Atkinson. 'But as you raised it, who threw it out the window?'

'I'll take over from here,' said Miss Luxton, who had silently slipped into the dorm. 'What's going on?'

'Miss, I saw the whole thing,' said Sasha. 'The new girl completely freaked out and threw her own pen out the window.'

'Yeah, I saw it too,' said Miranda.

'Did she throw it with her left hand?' asked Miss Atkinson. 'Because Ruby is left-handed you know.'

'Yes! It was *definitely* with her left hand,' said Sasha.

'I'm one hundred per cent sure it was her left hand too,' said Miranda.

'Oops, I made a mistake!' said Miss Atkinson. 'You're *right*-handed aren't you, Ruby?'

Ruby nodded as the young teacher gave her a supportive wink.

'Who cares which hand she used ...' said Miss Luxton.

'But—'

'What did I tell you about "buts" Miss Atkinson!'

'It proves these two are lying ...'

'My two best soccer players wouldn't lie, would you, girls?'

'No, Miss Luxton,' said Sasha and Miranda in sickly unison.

'Well, that's all settled,' said the boarding house mistress. 'Come along, Miss Atkinson, I need you to help me wash some soccer balls.'

'But—'

'No buts!'

As soon as the two teachers left, Sasha turned to Ruby.

'Serves you right for being a dobber!'

She then marched over to Ruby's desk, snatched a marker from the pencil case and picked up the sketch pad.

'Mmm, I think this lady needs a moustache!'

Ruby grabbed the pencil case out of Sasha's hand, then tried to get her pad back. But Sasha would not let go.

Rrrrrrrippppppppp!

The 'in-flight whining' drawing was suddenly torn in half. Sasha and Miranda started laughing hysterically, while the other two girls in the dorm looked away, pretending they hadn't noticed.

Ruby could feel a tear welling up in her eye, and dashed towards the door clutching her pencil case and pad.

'You won't even last as long as "Lame-o" Lane!' called Sasha after her.

As Ruby rushed from the dorm, she bumped into a short girl with a dark, untidy bob, who was coming the other way.

'Are you okay?' asked the girl, straightening her glasses.

Ruby was too upset to reply. She sprinted out of the boarding house and kept on running. She ran past the giant hedge, past an old maintenance shed and then headed towards the tall picket fence that separated the rear of Hetherington Hall from some thickly forested land.

On reaching the fence, Ruby stopped to get her breath back. Her heart was pounding as she glanced to her right and noticed a hole in some of the pickets. *An escape hatch!* She squeezed through the opening, then quickly sought the cover of the shrubs and trees.

Being out in the fresh air and surrounded by the lush greenery helped calm Ruby down. As she started walking, she ran her hand lightly over the ferns and the undergrowth. It reminded her of when she and her parents had lived in the country. On sunny afternoons they would pack a picnic lunch, go for long walks, and play 'I Spy'.

They were special times — back when her mum was normal and her dad was … alive.

A bit further on, she spotted a white object that was almost completely hidden behind some bushes. Ruby went over and pulled back the leaves to reveal a wooden sign that said 'LAND FOR SALE'. She shook her head. *How's anyone going to know it's for sale if they put the sign here?* she thought. She continued walking and eventually arrived at a small clearing with a large, smooth flat rock to sit on.

'Perfect!'

Ruby sat down, opened her sketch pad and looked around.

'Come on, inspire me,' she joked.

Out of the corner of her eye she picked up a colourful flash of movement. A bird had landed nearby and was now walking towards her.

'Aww, how cute!'

The bird was as vibrant as a rainbow, with a red face, a deep purple chest and patches of light blue, yellow and two different shades of green. Ruby cocked her head to one side, and the bird did exactly the same thing.

'So, what would you like me to call you?'

The small bird chirped a response.

'Okay, Chirpy it is.'

Ruby took out her pencils and started drawing Chirpy's distinctive colourful patches. She smiled as the bird paraded back and forth, like a fashion model on a catwalk.

'That's it, Chirpy! Work it!'

After finishing her sketch, Ruby added the caption: 'Chirpy — my new BFF!'

As she turned the page of her pad, a cartoon idea popped into her head. She quickly drew an embarrassed-looking bird with some angry cats on a modelling runway. At the bottom she wrote, 'Sorry, I thought this was a _BIRD_-walk!' She held it up to show her little friend who chirped enthusiastically.

'Yeah, Dad would have thought it was funny, too.'

She glanced at her watch and raised her eyebrows.

'Uh oh, dinner's in twenty minutes.'

Ruby closed her pad and waved goodbye to her striking new pal. As she started walking back towards the school, she noticed Chirpy following her.

'No way, Chirpy,' she said. 'You really don't want to meet Sasha!'

Ruby was relieved that her first day in the boarding house was almost over. She yawned as she flicked off the fluorescent light above her desk and dived into bed.

Instantly, she knew something was wrong. She tried to push her feet towards the end of the bed, but something was blocking them.

A chorus of snickering arose from around the dorm, as Ruby leapt back onto the polished wooden floor. Someone on the other side of the room jumped out of their bed and walked over. It was the small girl with glasses Ruby had bumped into earlier.

'Sasha short-sheeted your bed,' she said.

'You are such a little dobber, Pavlova!' complained Sasha.

'Short-sheeted?' said Ruby.

The girl pulled back the top sheet to reveal it had been doubled back over so that it looked like both the top and bottom sheets. The furthest Ruby's feet could have moved down the bed was less than halfway.

'I'm Fav, by the way,' said the girl. 'How about I give you a hand to fix it?'

'You're a total suck, Pavlova,' said Sasha. 'No wonder *everyone* hates you!'

'*I* don't hate you, Fav!' said Ruby, and they both burst out laughing.

'Laugh now, newbie,' hissed Sasha, 'because you *won't* be laughing tomorrow!'

CHAPTER

5

The next morning Ruby awoke to chaos.

Miss Luxton entered the dorm blowing her whistle, and girls started rushing everywhere, getting ready for the day. Ruby imagined this was what it looked like when the captain of a sinking vessel yelled, 'Abandon ship!'

After spending twenty minutes queuing up for a shower, she waited in line for another ten minutes before being let into the dining room. Once inside, she discovered there were unwritten rules about where she was allowed to sit.

'Don't even think about it!' said Sasha as Ruby approached her table.

'Or there!' called out Miranda as she was about to take a seat at another table.

'You're on the losers' table over there,' said Sasha, pointing to the far corner where Fav was sitting on her own. Ruby rolled her eyes and walked over to Fav with her breakfast tray.

'Private Loser reporting for duty, sir!' said Ruby, snapping to attention and giving a salute. Fav burst out laughing and pulled out a chair, as Sasha shot them a filthy look.

While they ate some rubbery scrambled eggs, Fav gave Ruby some valuable mealtime tips, like 'Never eat the sweet corn on Mondays if it was served the Friday before.'

After breakfast, Ruby returned to the dorm to get ready for her first class at Hetherington Hall. She checked her laptop and clicked on an email that had arrived from her mum.

Hey Rubes,

You've probably already made lots of friends, and hopefully the food is an improvement on my cooking! Dave is busy working on some big deal so it's pretty quiet here. He asked me to remind you to be good, as he called in a big favour to get you into Hetherington Hall.

Missing you,
Love Mum xx

Ruby's jaw tightened and she forcefully started typing a reply.

Hey Mum,
I h8 Hetherington Hall! The food is terrible, there r bul-
lies, & the boarding house mistress is a soccer nut who
doesn't like me.
I don't care about Dave and his stupid deals, so please
never mention him again.
Love (not!)
Ruby
P.S. I will <u>never</u> forgive u for sending me here.

Ruby read back her email, then took a deep calming breath. She quickly deleted what she had typed and replaced it with:

Hey Mum,
All good here. Got 2 get 2 class.
Love Rubes x

Ruby pushed send then stood up and inspected herself in the mirror on her cupboard door. Her brush had unsuccessfully tried to tame her wild hair and her new school uniform was at least a size too big.

Fav walked over with a grin on her face.

'Looking sharp!'

'Was just thinking the same thing,' said Ruby.

'Hey, do you know how to get to class?' asked Fav.

'Sure, we're in room 4303B, which is right next to room 4303A, yes?'

'Uh huh ... and do you know where room 4303A is?'

'Not a clue!'

Fav laughed so hard she snorted.

'How about I show you the way?'

Ruby sighed with relief. 'Thanks, Fav.'

'You won't be thanking me when you meet our teacher, Miss Vermin.'

Ruby swallowed hard and felt a sudden pang of nervousness in her stomach.

They both packed up their books and headed out of the boarding house.

'Most of our classes are with Miss Vermin, unfortunately,' explained Fav. 'She teaches English, geography and history ...'

Ruby stopped. She thought she heard something whistling through the air.

Splat!

She was suddenly drenched in water and could hear raucous laughter coming from above. She looked up as the smirking faces of Sasha and Miranda quickly disappeared from a window on the second floor. On the ground at her feet were two empty, sodden plastic bags.

'Water bombs,' said Fav. 'You okay?'

'I've been drier,' replied Ruby.

'Let's go back so you can get changed.'

The girls turned around but their path was blocked by a tall, balding man in an academic gown. He had a pale face, a receding hairline and a disapproving frown. Ruby had no idea where he had come from but was sure she had seen him before. Then she remembered. *The man with the photoshopped smile ... Headmaster Lemon!*

The headmaster looked Ruby up and down and shook his head.

'Miss West, I presume?'

Ruby nodded nervously.

'In a water fight on your first day,' he continued. 'I'm guessing you're a troublemaker with a capital T. What do you have to say about that?'

Ruby was too frightened to speak, and stared at the ground in silence.

'What do you think, Miss Sharma?' said the headmaster, pointing at Fav.

'Well, I'm pretty sure "troublemaker" should only have a capital T if it's the first word in the sentence. Or if someone's name was actually Troublemaker ... although, it would be pretty weird for parents to call their kid Troublemaker, so ...'

'That's not what I meant!' roared Mr Lemon.

Ruby had to bite her tongue to stop herself from laughing.

'I'm putting you on notice, Miss West,' he said. 'And I'll be watching you like a hawk!'

'Why a hawk?' asked Fav.

Mr Lemon looked slightly puzzled, then said, 'Because they have the best eyesight of all the birds.'

'No, that would be the eagle,' explained Fav.

'Well, hawks have the *second*-best eyesight, so …'

'I'd argue owls would be in second place; their night vision is amaz—'

'It doesn't matter what sort of stupid bird I am!' exploded the headmaster. 'Miss West, all you need to know is that I'm watching you, and if you do *one* thing wrong I'm going to pounce!'

'Like a tiger?' asked Ruby.

'Yes, like a …'

Realizing how foolish he sounded, Mr Lemon abruptly stopped speaking and stormed off in a huff.

When he was gone, Fav held up her hands as if they were claws and said, 'Like a *tiger*!'

They both burst out laughing.

Despite being located inside an old sandstone building, room 4303B turned out to be a very modern classroom. It had stark white walls, well-spaced desks and an expensive-looking interactive whiteboard.

'Sorry we're late, Miss Vermin,' said Fav as she and Ruby walked in.

The boys and girls all turned and gawked at Ruby, instantly making her face redden. To make matters worse, she spotted Sasha and Miranda, who were both pretending to throw water bombs at her.

'Being a scholarship student, I expected more from you, Faviola,' said the teacher seated at the front of the class. 'And Ruby, this is not a good start! You can take Molly's old spot over there.'

Miss Vermin had dark brown hair tied up in a tight bun, and she sported a pair of light blue tinted glasses. She was wearing earrings that did not appear to match, as well as an excessive amount of eyeshadow, rouge and lipstick.

I've seen clowns with less make-up, thought Ruby as she moved towards her seat.

'Phwoar!' yelled out Sasha as Ruby walked by.

'What's going on?' demanded Miss Vermin.

'Ruby did a bad smell, Miss,' said Sasha. 'I think we should call her 'Poo-by', not Ruby!'

The class erupted with laughter.

'Ha! Poo-by!' cackled Miranda. 'Because she let one rip and her name's Ruby!'

'Wow! Did you work that out all by yourself?' said Fav, rolling her eyes.

'Are you calling me stupid?' growled Miranda.

'No,' said Fav. 'I'm calling you vacuous.'

'Well the joke's on you, Pavlova,' said Miranda. 'Because I don't even own a vacuum!'

'Enough! All of you!' screeched the teacher as Ruby sat down and tried to make herself invisible. Miss Vermin scowled at her new student, then started writing up some questions on the whiteboard.

'Pssst!'

Ruby turned around and saw that Sasha was trying to get her attention.

'Guess what I've got planned for you at recess, Poo-by!'

'A surprise party?' whispered back Ruby with a fake smile.

'How come you're giving *her* a surprise party?' asked Miranda.

Sasha shot her friend a withering look, then turned back to Ruby.

'It's not a party, Poo-by, but it will be fun. I've made up a list of nicknames to call you. The first one's Toad-face, but after that they get a lot worse!'

'Who cares …'

'Face the front and stop talking, Ruby!' squawked Miss Vermin.

'Yeah, Poo-by! Some of us are trying to work,' said Sasha.

'Any more disruptions, Miss West, and you'll stay back after school.'

Ruby's shoulders slumped and she let out a deep sigh. Within her first twenty-four hours at Hetherington Hall, she had been called nasty names, been waterbombed and had her bed short-sheeted. The bullies seemed to have the teachers wrapped around their little fingers and, worst of all, her special pen had been thrown away.

She fought back a tear as she unzipped her alligator pencil case and peered inside. Suddenly Ruby froze. She blinked a few times to make sure she wasn't seeing things. Sitting among her pencils and markers … was the battered old pen.

Ruby carefully pulled it out and rolled it around in her hand. Straight away, her anxiety was replaced by a warm, glowing feeling that shot up through the tips of her fingers and surged throughout her whole body.

'Nothing can harm me,' she whispered.

Without realizing what she was doing, Ruby grabbed a piece of paper and started doodling. It was as if she was in a dream. A nice dream. A safe dream …

'Ruby, I'm waiting for an answer!'

Miss Vermin's nasally voice snapped Ruby back into the real world.

'Um, sorry, Miss, I'm not sure …'

'What? You don't know the capital of Scotland? It's even written on the board! Clearly *you're* not here on a scholarship!'

The class erupted in laughter once again.

'Miss, if Ruby had a brain cell, it would be lonely!' called out Sasha.

Most of the class laughed again, including Miss Vermin, who was pointing to the word 'Edinburgh' on the whiteboard.

'The answer is of course, "En-din-burra" …'

Fav's hand shot up, and Miss Vermin rolled her eyes.

'Yes, Faviola.'

'It's pronounced "Ed-in-burra" not "En-din-burra".'

'Really?' said Miss Vermin. 'Well um … who cares? It's not as if anyone important came from there …'

A solid boy with curly red hair immediately raised his hand, causing Miss Vermin to sigh.

'Yes, Dougal.'

'What about Alexander Graham Bell?'

'Huh?'

'The guy who invented the telephone; he was born in Edinburgh,' explained Dougal.

'Oh … but he's the *only* famous person born there,' said Miss Vermin dismissively.

'Robert Louis Stevenson,' pointed out Fav.

'Who?'

'He wrote *Treasure Island* and—'

'Well … he's no J.K. Rowling, is he?' interrupted the teacher.

'Do you know where J.K. Rowling lives?' asked Dougal.

'No,' replied Miss Vermin.

'Edinburgh!' said Dougal and Fav together.

Ruby burst out laughing and the teacher glared at her.

'You have just earned yourself a detention!'

Miss Vermin turned back to the whiteboard and Ruby shook her head before glancing down at her desk.

She immediately raised her eyebrows, as sitting in front of her was a drawing. It was definitely her style, but she could not remember sketching it. It was a girl's face, with flowing hair and a nose that had a small pimple on the end of it. In her handwriting, underneath it, were the words, 'She's gonna blow!' Ruby looked at the eyes in the drawing. They were cruel, just like …

She slowly turned around and peeked at Sasha. There was

something slightly different about her …

'Look at me again and you'll regret it!' hissed Sasha.

Ruby faced the front of class for the rest of the lesson, and when the bell for recess finally sounded she let out a huge sigh of relief. Even though Sasha was about to bombard her with a range of horrible names, she didn't care now that her pen was back.

Ruby remained in her seat and watched Miranda slowly walk over to Sasha with her mouth wide open.

'What are you staring at?' demanded Sasha.

'Um … your nose … you kinda got, um, a bit of a … pimple …' stammered Miranda.

'I don't get pimples! My family all have perfect skin …'

Sasha reached up to feel her nose and touched what looked more like a golf ball than a pimple. A look of terror appeared on her face and she bolted out the door.

Miranda glanced down at Ruby's desk and noticed her drawing. She looked

BLOW!!!

at Ruby quizzically, before racing off to join her friend in the bathroom opposite the classroom.

Ruby followed in hot pursuit and, after opening the bathroom door, spotted Sasha staring at the mirror in a state of shock. The pimple on her nose was now the size of a softball!

Sasha let out a high-pitched scream that could be heard all around Hetherington Hall.

'Arghhhhhhhhhhhhhhhhhhhhhhhhhhhhhhhhh!'

Unfortunately, the high pitch of her scream was enough to set off the bulging pimple. Ruby watched in astonishment as the giant zit exploded, covering the mirror, Sasha and Miranda in disgusting yellow pus.

CHAPTER

6

Hetherington Hall was buzzing with talk about Sasha's exploding pimple. As Ruby and Fav walked to soccer training, they overheard two younger boys discussing the rumours.

'I heard the groundsman had to wear a hazchem suit to clean the bathroom!'

'Well, Jeremy Rundle reckons when the zit burst, spiders came out!' said the other boy.

'Are you sure?'

'Yeah! As if Jeremy Rundle would make that up!'

Ruby decided not to believe a word Jeremy Rundle said if she ever met him.

She looked across at Fav and asked a question that had been gnawing away at her since she arrived.

'Hey, what happened to Molly Lane?'

Fav frowned then took a deep breath.

'Sasha gave her a hard time, and no one — including me

— stood up for her … especially at the start.'

Fav shook her head before continuing.

'Everyone was too scared to do anything, as they didn't want Sasha to pick on them too. I finally stood up for Molly, but … it was too late. She rang her parents in tears one night, and they came and took her away.'

'At least you tried to help her,' said Ruby. 'What I don't understand is why nearly everyone at this school is so mean.'

'I blame the headmaster,' replied Fav. 'He's rude and nasty, and that rubs off onto some of the teachers and then to the students.'

'Why don't the good teachers say something?'

'They do. But then Mr Lemon doesn't renew their teaching contracts at the end of the year,' explained Fav.

'And he lets Miss Luxton and Miss Vermin get away with being mean because they'll do anything he says,' Ruby added.

'Exactly! You are *so* much smarter than what Miss Vermin tells everyone,' said Fav cheekily.

'Ouch!' said Ruby with a smile. 'Anyway, thanks for sticking up for me.'

'You would have done the same for me …'

'No way!' said Ruby.

The two friends laughed as a shrill blast from a whistle sliced through the air.

'Everybody in!' yelled Miss Luxton.

Girls ran from everywhere on the Raleigh-Hinds oval and formed a tight huddle around their coach. Ruby ended up standing near Sasha, who was wearing a sticky plaster on her swollen nose.

Sasha started whispering to Miranda, and Ruby leaned closer to listen in.

'... so I rang Mum's plastic surgeon and she doesn't think it will scar permanently, which is such a relief. I still have no idea how I got a pimple.'

'Yeah, about that,' said Miranda. 'You're going to think this is weird, but I saw this drawing and—'

'Stop gas-bagging, Miranda!' called out Miss Luxton. 'We're going to start with some basic dribbling skills ...'

'Fav, what's dribbling?' whispered Ruby.

'Ha!' said Fav. Then she looked at Ruby. 'Wait. You're serious, aren't you?'

Ruby nodded. 'Is "dribbling" anything like drooling? Hope not — I had this really bad experience on the plane ...'

'Ruby!' yelled Miss Luxton. 'You obviously think you're an expert, so you can go first to show us how it's done.'

'But—'

'No buts! I want you to dribble the ball around the cones, and do the same on the way back, then pass the ball to the girl at the front of the line. Got it?'

Ruby stared blankly at the coach.

'Dribble means running along and kicking the ball to yourself,' whispered Fav.

'Thanks!'

When Miss Luxton kicked the ball firmly along the ground towards her, Ruby had no idea what to do. So she did nothing. The steamrolling soccer ball hit the tips of her sneakers and ricocheted into her chin. Everyone burst out laughing apart from Fav and Miss Luxton, who shook her head in dismay.

'I'm trying to work out what's worse,' said Sasha. 'Poo-by's soccer skills or her haircut … let's call it a nil all draw!'

This caused another outbreak of laughter.

The ball had dropped down at Ruby's feet, and she gritted her teeth and stared at the intimidating line of orange cones. She remembered some advice Bertie had once given her, after she refused to try his homemade nougat: 'You'll never know, if you don't have a go!' She had cautiously taken a nibble and discovered it was deliciously soft and chewy.

Maybe soccer will be deliciously soft and chewy too! she thought.

As she prepared to dribble the ball through the cones, the boys' team walked by on their way to practise on the adjacent oval. *No pressure!*

She took a deep breath, then tentatively kicked the ball a short distance in front of her. A small smile appeared on her face. *That was pretty easy.*

She did it again as she approached the first cone. *Nice! You got this Rubes. You got—*

Ruby suddenly tripped over the ball and landed face first on the ground.

There was lots of laughter from both teams, but also a few concerned 'oooh's.

Fortunately, Ruby wasn't hurt and she immediately leapt back to her feet. The first thing she saw was Sasha and Miranda pointing and laughing at her, and she remembered some other advice her dad had passed on: 'No one can laugh at you if you can laugh at yourself.'

Ruby smiled and called out, 'Thank you, thank you! And now for my next trick … I'll make this soccer ball disappear!' She picked up the soccer ball, looked around slyly, then stuffed it underneath her top.

'Ta dah!' she said with a magician's flourish.

All the students, apart from Sasha and Miranda, laughed and gave her a huge round of applause.

Miss Luxton gave three blasts of her whistle and put her hands on her hips until everyone was silent.

'Ruby, for your own safety and everyone else's, go and practise by yourself on the other side of the oval.'

But instead of being embarrassed by the putdown, Ruby nodded and said, 'Great call, Miss Luxton.' This led to another round of laughter and another blast of the whistle.

Ruby took the ball out from under her top and jogged towards the edge of the oval. She was wondering if Miss Luxton ate soccer balls for breakfast when a deep voice called out to her.

'How's it going, Ruby?'

It was Mr Chol, who she guessed was the coach of the boys' team. Ruby waved and held up the ball.

'Good thanks. Just practising my … dribble.'

He gave her a grin and returned to coaching his team. Ruby shook her head. *The boys get Mr Chol and we get Miss Luxton … so not fair!*

Right on cue, she heard the piercing sound of a whistle followed by Miss Luxton yelling out, 'Come on, Faviola, I've seen sloths try harder than you!' Ruby smiled, as the mention of sloths gave her an idea for a cartoon. She pictured a frightened woman standing next to a bomb saying, 'It's set to explode in ten seconds!' The Bomb Disposal Officer, who just happens to be a sloth replies, 'Sorry, I'm on my break.'

She arrived at the edge of the oval and spotted the solid kid with curly red hair from her class.

'Hey, Dougal,' she called out.

Dougal smiled and said, 'It's Ruby, yeah?'

Ruby smiled back and said, 'Yep … although some people pronounce it "Poo-by"!'

'Ha! You mean Sasha! You may not know this, but she has a serious problem with her heart …'

Ruby paused. 'No, I didn't know,' she said.

'Yeah … she doesn't have one!'

Dougal burst out laughing and Ruby immediately joined in.

'You totally had me!' she said. 'I was even feeling sorry for her!'

Ruby pointed to a small, black rectangular box in Dougal's hands.

'What's that?'

'My drone remote control,' he said.

She looked up and saw a drone cruising around above the players.

'Awesome.'

'Yeah, Mr Chol gets me to film the training sessions and the games, and he uses the footage to help teach the players about tactics.'

Ruby looked on as Dougal made the drone zip all over the place with subtle movements of the transmitter's throttle.

'Can you make that thing deliver pizzas?' she asked, causing Dougal to chuckle.

Ruby spotted one of the soccer boys jogging towards them. He had thick wavy hair, deep brown eyes and he moved as smoothly as a panther. He flashed a smile at Ruby and she automatically smiled back.

'That was the best face plant I've ever seen,' he said.

Ruby went bright red.

'Thanks for bringing up the most embarrassing moment of my life!'

'Don't be embarrassed! It was seriously cool the way you owned it,' said the boy. 'I'm Andre by the way.'

'I'm Ruby … Ruby McClutzville.'

Andre burst out laughing and over his shoulder Ruby could see Sasha giving her a filthy look. *I am so going to get it!*

CHAPTER

7

The next morning before she left for school, Ruby sat down at her desk and opened her laptop to check for emails. As she waited for her computer to fire up, she glanced down at her feet and winced.

'New school shoes are the worst!' she grumbled. She took them off, placed them at the end of her bed, then went back to her laptop. A familiar 'ping' announced that a message had come through.

Hey Rubes,
Your email was short and sweet, but I'm sure you're busy hanging out with all your new friends. Very quiet here — Dave is working long hours and still won't let me near his Porsche (except to wash it) but says if this big deal he's working on comes off, he'll take us somewhere special next school holidays.

Have a great day!
Love Mum xx

Ruby screwed up her face and started typing.

Hey Mum,
Your email made me smile. All my new friends? I only
have 1 — 2 if u count birds! If Dave cares more about
his car than u, then maybe he's trying 2 tell u something?
Oh, and by the way, I would rather stay in my room
without food than holiday with him. Have a gr8 day?
LOL! No chance thanks to Sasha.
Must head to school now — fun day ahead!
Love,
Rubes x

Ruby slumped back in her chair and shook her head.

'You ready Rubes?' called out Fav from the other side of
the dorm.

'Just a sec!'

Ruby leaned forward and deleted most of the email so
that it now read:

Hey Mum,
Your email made me smile.
Must head to school now — fun day ahead!
Love,
Rubes x

She pushed send and raced over to put on her shoes, but stopped when she realized someone had fastened the laces together in a huge, tight knot.

'Looks like you might be *tied up* for a while!' mocked Sasha from the doorway.

'Tied up? … Oh, because of the shoelaces — good one!' said Miranda.

Sasha rolled her eyes as the two bullies exited the dorm.

'You go ahead Fav, I'll see you in class,' said Ruby.

'You sure?'

'No point both of us getting into trouble.'

After Fav left, Ruby grabbed a pen from her desk and began to prise the irritating knot loose. To her surprise it unravelled fairly easily, and after a quick dash to school she arrived at the classroom before Miss Vermin. *Phew!*

As she walked through the door, she overheard Sasha say, 'Shh, here she comes!'

The class was eerily quiet as Ruby moved towards her seat;

nobody said a word. Some kids stared at her with a smirk, while others overtly avoided eye contact.

A nervous shiver went up her spine as she slowly sat down.

Suddenly Fav called out in a strange, clipped voice, 'Hey — Ruby — what — is — up?'

'Good on you, Pavlova. Spoil a really good joke!' said Sasha.

She then pointed at Fav and said, 'Now *you're* "silenced" for twenty-four hours as well!'

'Silenced?' mouthed Ruby with a shake of her head.

The room went quiet for a few seconds before Dougal stood up and said,

'Hey — Ruby — hey — Fav — I — too — ask — what — is — up?'

'All three of you are officially "silenced" until 9 a.m. tomorrow!' yelled Sasha. 'No one talks to these losers until then!'

Fav shrugged her shoulders. 'Gee, Sasha not talking to us for a whole day ... how are we going to cope?' Ruby and Dougal burst out laughing, and Sasha looked set to explode, but Miss Vermin arrived before she could say anything. *I never thought I'd be glad to see Miss Vermin!* thought Ruby.

A few minutes later, Ruby glanced back and spotted Sasha writing a note. Sasha passed it on to the boy next to her, and eventually Miranda tossed it onto Ruby's desk.

'Don't give it to *her*!' hissed Sasha.

Ruby opened up the note and read the message. *Poo-by, Pavlova and the Ginger are all loser freaks! Pass it on.*

Ruby's nostrils instantly flared, and without realizing it, she reached into her pencil case and pulled out her special pen. The familiar surge of warm energy flowed into the tips of her fingers, then spread throughout her body.

'Nothing can harm me,' she whispered as she slipped into a nice, safe daydream …

'Who can answer that?'

Miss Vermin's annoying voice woke Ruby up, and she immediately looked down at her desk. *Another drawing!*

It was Sasha's face again, but this time her mouth was 'zipped up' and there was a clock in the background showing 9 a.m. At the bottom were the words, '24 hours of *bliss!*'

'If no one volunteers, I'll pick someone at random!' threatened Miss Vermin.

Ruby looked up at her teacher and started to panic. *Please don't pick me, please don't pick me …*

'Yes, Sasha,' said Miss Vermin.

Ruby exhaled quietly and turned to listen to Sasha's answer. But just as the bully started to speak, a buzzing fly darted into her mouth.

Initially her voice sounded like Donald Duck, then it completely disappeared.

'Can't talk!' she mouthed to Miss Vermin.

'Miranda, take Sasha down to the sick bay,' said the teacher.

'Yes, Miss,' said Miranda, who glanced at Ruby's desk as she walked by.

She stopped and stared open mouthed at the drawing, before rushing to help her friend out of the classroom.

At lunchtime Ruby sat at the 'losers' table in the dining room with Fav and Dougal. She was staring at her meal, trying to work out if it was an Irish stew or an attempted shepherd's pie that had gone horribly wrong when Dougal interrupted her thoughts.

'Rubes, don't you think it's strange that after you drew a picture of Sasha with a zipped-up mouth, she suddenly lost her voice?'

'Yeah, and when you drew Sasha with a pimple, bang! She immediately grows a massive one,' added Fav.

'Massive?' said Dougal. 'I could have landed my drone on that thing!'

Ruby laughed and pulled out her pen.

'It's just a weird coincidence, and I'll prove it,' she said. 'Who is the worst soccer player you know?'

'Well … you are,' said Fav.

'Easily!' added Dougal with a chuckle. 'It's not even close.'

'Thanks! So how about I draw myself scoring a goal in Saturday's game?'

'Yeah, that *is* pretty unlikely!' said Fav.

As Ruby started to doodle, she once again felt the surge of warmth spreading through her body. But it felt different this time. *This time I'm more in control,* she thought.

As she inspected her sketch, an idea popped into her head. She smiled as she made one last addition.

'And here's Sasha … and because she calls me Poo-by … here's a bird … dropping a poo on *her* head!'

'Okay, that definitely won't happen, but it is very funny!' said Dougal.

Ruby sensed someone peering over her shoulder and turned around to see Miranda lurking in the background.

'I wonder if she saw your cartoon?' asked Fav.

'Who cares?' said Ruby. 'It's just a stupid drawing.'

Ruby was reading a Ms. Marvel comic on her bed after school, when she heard Sasha approaching along the corridor.

'Where's Poo-by?'

Great, she's got her voice back! thought Ruby.

Sasha had been in the sick bay for three days. *Three beautiful days.*

Ruby quickly thought through her options.

I could be brave and stay here, or … She leapt off her bed and hid in her cupboard.

'Aww, Poo-by's not here!' moaned Sasha. 'Pity, as I thought up some catchy new nicknames for her while I was sick.'

Ruby carefully pushed the cupboard door open by about a centimetre, so she could hear more clearly.

'How did you get your voice back?' asked Miranda.

'That stupid fly suddenly flew out my mouth, and straight away I could speak again.'

'Um, was that at about 9 o'clock this morning?' asked Miranda nervously.

'How did you know that?'

'Well Ruby, I mean Poo-by, did this drawing of you with a zipper on your mouth and it had a clock that said 9 a.m. …'

'You can be *so* thick sometimes, Miranda …'

'But she also did one of you with a pimple, like, just before you got the … pimple.'

'Really?'

'And she's done another drawing, where she scores a goal tomorrow, and a bird drops poo on your head.'

Sasha started laughing uncontrollably.

'Poo-by kick a goal? That's like you winning the maths prize! She has no chance of scoring and who cares if a bit of bird poo ends up in my hair? I've got this amazing one-hundred-dollar shampoo that Kim Kardashian uses …'

Ruby heard the bullies' voices trail off as they left the dorm, and cautiously crept out of the cupboard.

She folded her arms as she considered what Sasha had just said.

Maybe I could kick a goal tomorrow! Ruby pretended to kick a make-believe soccer ball, and stubbed her toe on the floor.

Ouch! Maybe not.

CHAPTER

It was a beautiful Saturday morning at Hetherington Hall, with the sun shining majestically in the cloudless light blue sky. Ruby stared at the Monsetto Grammar girls in their red and black uniforms on the other side of the Raleigh-Hinds oval. They looked nothing like the brutish thugs Miss Vermin had described at training.

The coach split the Hetherington players into pairs to do some stretching, and Ruby's partner was Fav.

'So how are you going to kick your goal today, Rubes? A penalty? A shot from outside the box?'

'Outside the what?' asked Ruby.

Miss Vermin blew her whistle and instructed the players to do some simple pre-match drills. Ruby managed to mis-kick the ball in every single one of them.

'At least you're consistent,' muttered the coach.

Ruby glanced over at Sasha, and smiled when she saw her

looking up at the sky. *I can't believe she's taking my drawing seriously …*

'Look out!'

Ruby heard the call too late and a ball thumped into the back of her head.

'Are you okay?' asked Fav. 'There's some ice behind the coach's box if you need it.'

Ruby felt fine, but she was sick of embarrassing herself.

'Thanks, Fav,' she said, holding the back of her head. 'I might go grab some.'

Ruby went over and lay down behind the coach's box where no one could see her. It was so cosy in the warm sun that she almost dozed off, but her drowsiness was interrupted by some voices on the other side of the coach's box.

'Hey, Miss Luxton.'

'Hi, Sasha. Glad you got your voice back. We had no chance today without you.'

'Thanks, and just so you know, *I* think you're a great coach …'

'Thanks … hey, why did you say that?'

'It's … don't worry, I don't want to get Ruby, I mean, someone else in trouble.'

Ruby rolled her eyes. *No one's going to fall for that …*

'What did Ruby say?'

… except Miss Luxton!

'Not much … just that a trained seal would be a better coach, and its breath would smell much nicer.'

'Unbelievable! Ruby definitely won't be playing today.'

Miss Luxton blew her whistle and screamed, 'Everyone in!'

As the last girls arrived, Ruby slipped out from behind the coach's box and joined the rest of the team.

'One of you has been talking behind my back,' said the coach dramatically. 'So *Ruby*, you will be sitting on the bench … all day!'

Instead of being angry, Ruby was thrilled. This would prove once and for all that Fav and Dougal's theory about the pen was ridiculous. *Pretty hard to kick a goal if you're not playing!*

The boys' team was competing on the next oval, and Ruby waved to Dougal as he prepared to film the game with his drone. He smiled and manoeuvred his flying machine so that it hovered above her head.

'Aww, it's saying hello,' she said, giving a wave.

'Get that thing away from here!' thundered Miss Luxton.

The drone suddenly lunged at the coach, forcing her to dive onto the ground.

'Sorry — finger slipped!' called out Dougal.

Chapter 8

Miss Luxton angrily jumped back to her feet, but was distracted by the blast of the referee's whistle, signalling the game was about to start.

Ruby looked on as the match began at a frenzied pace. The Hetherington left full-back rolled her ankle in the first minute.

'Great! One of my best players is out for the game,' grumbled Miss Luxton.

A short time later another Hetherington player went down with a nasty cut to her leg.

'She'll need stitches,' said the referee.

'What next?' cried Miss Luxton.

Just as Miss Luxton said that, two of her midfielders collided and lay on the ground holding their heads.

'Better have them checked for concussion,' said one of the parents.

'But, but—' stammered the coach.

No buts, Miss Luxton, thought Ruby.

At half-time, the score was still nil all, and Ruby noticed there were now only two other players left on the bench.

'Our luck has to change,' said a frazzled Miss Luxton as she addressed her team during the break.

But as soon as the second half began, the team's run of misfortune continued. The goalkeeper felt a sharp pain in her stomach and then a defender pulled her hamstring.

There was now only one person on the bench … Ruby.

With five minutes to go, the score was still nil all. That was when a Hetherington player crashed into the goal post, dislocating her shoulder.

'Nooooo!' screamed Miss Luxton.

As the poor girl was helped from the ground, the coach looked over at Ruby and stamped her foot.

'I'll probably regret this … but you're on.'

Ruby decided it was best to stay away from the action, so she ran to the far side of the pitch. She looked across at the neighbouring oval just as Andre kicked an amazing goal for the boys' team. As the boys high-fived each other to celebrate, Ruby noticed one of her sneakers was undone, and bent down to tie up her laces. Right at that moment Sasha had the ball in defence, and decided to kick it as hard as she could up the field. The ball flew off her boot like a low flying missile. It hit an unsuspecting Ruby on the top of her head, ricocheted forty metres, and completely bamboozled the Monsetto goalkeeper.

As the ball bounced into the back of the net, Miss Luxton yelled out, 'Yeeeeeeeeessssss!'

The siren sounded, and the Hetherington players rushed over to congratulate Ruby on her miraculous 'header' goal.

As her teammates jumped up and down and gave her hugs, she spotted Sasha standing on her own. Her arms were folded and she had a sour look on her face. Ruby grinned. *Where's the love?*

A giant shadow suddenly appeared around Sasha, and she automatically looked up. It was a bird … a big one! Sasha's mouth opened in shock, as an enormous pelican dumped a steaming pile of poo on her.

Ruby was at least thirty metres away, but the disgusting smell carried to her instantly. She screwed up her nose and thought, *Even Kim Kardashian's shampoo won't get that out!*

The old groundsman, who was touching up the boundary lines with white paint, shook his head.

'That's strange,' he said. 'Pelicans haven't been spotted around here for over sixty years.'

Fav, Dougal, Sasha and Miranda all stared at Ruby, and she knew exactly what they were thinking.

OMG. The pen really works!

CHAPTER

9

Ruby and Fav watched the groundsman hosing down Sasha in the middle of the oval.

'He was right about pelicans not having been here for ages,' said Fav. 'There's no body of water to support them.'

'Which means?'

'That pen must have amazing powers …'

Ruby noticed a large number of students were pointing at Sasha and laughing. The school bully's shoulders were slumped, her face was flushed and she was staring miserably at the ground.

'At least she won't be picking on us for a while,' said Ruby.

Fav frowned and rubbed her chin.

'Rubes, do you think that pen could be a little … dangerous?'

'Come on, Fav!' said Ruby. 'The girl who has given us, *and* Molly Lane, a really hard time is having pelican poo washed off her in public … can't you just enjoy the moment?'

'I suppose so,' said Fav with a reluctant smile.

Ruby gave her friend a nudge and decided to change the topic.

'Hey, how come you know so much about pelicans?'

'Birds are my hobby. Like, did you know some ducks sleep with one eye open? And chickens have over two hundred distinct noises for communicating, and …'

Ruby smiled and did a subtle eye roll. *Sorry I asked!*

That afternoon, Ruby snuck off to the land behind the school to draw cartoons and catch up with Chirpy.

But when she arrived at the clearing, her colourful friend was nowhere to be seen.

'Chirp, chirp. Chirp, chirp. Chirp, chirp.'

As soon as Ruby started chirping, the beautiful bird appeared as if by magic.

'Hey, Chirpy! Did you hear about my winning goal?'

The little bird looked at Ruby and started chirping.

'It was not a fluke!'

The bird chirped again.

'Okay, so it might have been a *bit* of a fluke.'

Chirpy jumped up and down and chirped even louder.

'All right! It was a *total* fluke. Sheesh, Chirpy, let it go!'

Ruby looked around and smiled. She loved the intermittent sound of the birds, the gentle movement of the trees swaying in the breeze, and the way the shadows silently crept forward.

She sighed contentedly, pulled out a pencil and started a drawing. Her drawing was inspired by what had happened to Sasha, and featured a statue of a nervous-looking pigeon, with humans flying above it. Down the bottom she wrote, 'Revenge!'

After finishing the drawing, Ruby looked at her watch and then at Chirpy.

'Better get back to the boarding house, my fine feathered friend.' She stood up, waved goodbye and started walking towards the fence. As she ambled along, she spotted a giant pine tree with thick, coarse branches and lush green pine needles. Years ago, her father had built her a cubby house in a similar tree. It had looked like a real house, with windows, a roof and a front door you climbed up to on a rope ladder. She would invite her parents over for morning tea, and Adelaide always laughed when Bertie sampled one of Ruby's 'delicious' mud pies.

Suddenly Ruby stopped reminiscing.

Mr Lemon!

She quickly dropped to the ground and crawled behind

the pine tree. She wasn't sure if she'd been spotted, so she waited thirty seconds before carefully peeking around the base of the tree.

Her eyes widened. The headmaster was poking around in the bushes where the real estate sign was hidden, and he was whistling!

About a minute later Ruby watched him stroll off, and he was *still* whistling. She waited until she was sure he was gone, then went over and pulled back the foliage. The real estate sign now had a bright red 'SOLD' sticker on it.

As Ruby stared at the sign, some unsettling questions jumped into her head. *Who bought the land? What are they going to do with it? And why is Mr Lemon so happy?*

Just as the girls were hopping into bed that night, Miss Luxton rushed into the dorm blowing her whistle.

'Big news!'

Ruby wondered what could have made the boarding house mistress so excited. *Maybe a new shipment of soccer balls has arrived?*

'Listen up!' said Miss Luxton. 'A journalist from the *Hetherington Herald* wants to interview some of our soccer players.'

'Cool!' said Sasha. 'When do they want to interview me?'

'Um, she doesn't want to interview *you* …'

'But … I'm the captain!'

'Yes, but the story is about the players who scored the winning goals on the weekend. Andre Amano and … Ruby.'

Ruby's jaw dropped.

'The interview is on Monday at 10.30 a.m. on the Raleigh-Hinds oval, and Ruby …' Miss Luxton put on a pathetic smile before she continued, '… you will say nice things about me, won't you?'

Ruby nodded politely, even though her fingers were crossed behind her back.

'Great! And if they ask, my first name is Bev. I hate Beverley so make sure you say Bev, got it?'

'Got it,' said Ruby.

As Ruby walked onto the Raleigh-Hinds oval, Andre waved and flashed a warm smile. Ruby panicked and gave him an extremely awkward return wave, making them both laugh.

Andre was standing next to a friendly-looking young woman with long dark hair who was wearing a white blouse, black pants and a matching black jacket.

'You must be Ruby West,' she said enthusiastically. 'I'm

Rosemary Arrow from the *Hetherington Herald.*'

'Hey,' said Ruby.

'I'll take a few photos, interview Andre, and then I'll talk to you. Cool?'

'Cool.'

The reporter positioned Ruby and Andre next to each other, then started taking some photos.

All of a sudden, she stopped and said, 'Ruby, you are allowed to breathe, you know!'

Ruby exhaled deeply and they all burst out laughing. She felt a lot more relaxed after that and could not stop smiling as the rest of the shots were taken. Rosemary then took out a small notepad and began interviewing Andre, while Ruby listened intently, hoping to pick up some tips.

'... I looked for a teammate, because our coach always says "pass to a player in a better position", but everyone was covered so I took the shot and luckily it curled into the top right corner. But the goal was set up by the defensive pressure of our players up the ground, so the whole team deserves the credit ...'

Ruby closed her eyes. *Compared to Andre, I am going to sound like a complete doofus!*

'That was great, Andre,' said Rosemary. 'Okay, Ruby, tell us about *your* winning goal.'

Ruby opened her eyes and swallowed. She felt like a kid about to sit a test, who hadn't done their homework.

'Um, the truth is … I was kind of distracted, and I was tying up my shoelaces, and I didn't see the ball coming, and it sort of accidentally bounced off my head, and I don't think the goal keepery person, or whatever they're called, was expecting it, and it just sailed past them into the big netty thing.'

Rosemary and Andre stared at Ruby, then suddenly cracked up laughing.

'That is the *best* goal-scoring story ever!' said the reporter.

'Brilliant!' said Andre.

'You have made my day, Ruby,' said Rosemary. 'Both goals sounded amazing — it's a pity no one filmed them.'

'Someone did,' said Andre. 'One of the students had a drone.'

'Do you think I'd be able to get the footage? Then our online readers can check them out.'

'I'll chat to Dougal Marshman, and if you give me your address, he can email it through,' said Andre.

'Awesome,' said Rosemary, handing Andre her business card. 'Oh, one last thing, can you give me your coaches' names so I can put them in the article?'

'Sure, Marley Chol,' said Andre.

'And the girls' coach?'

'*Beverley* Luxton,' replied Ruby with a smile.

Ruby and Andre said goodbye to Rosemary, then began chatting as they walked back to their respective classes.

'I wanted to ask you a favour,' said Andre.

'You don't want me to donate a kidney, do you?'

'Nothing like that!' laughed Andre. 'I'm the editor of this year's school magazine … and wondered if you'd be interested in doing some drawings to make it a bit more exciting?'

A puzzled expression appeared on Ruby's face.

'Sorry, I should have explained,' said Andre. 'Miss Atkinson told Mr Chol how amazing your cartoons are, and he told me.'

Ruby's heart started pounding as she was overcome by an unfamiliar feeling of pride.

They arrived at a long corridor near the quadrangle and stopped while Ruby considered Andre's offer.

'Hey, I totally understand if you don't …'

'I'd love to do it.'

'Thanks,' said Andre with a warm smile. 'You can draw whatever you like — I really want to shake things up.'

Their conversation was interrupted by a stern voice coming from the other end of corridor.

'Oi! Why aren't you two in class?'

'Oh no, of all the people,' whispered Ruby.

The headmaster started walking rapidly in their direction and Ruby braced herself for the inevitable detention.

Mr Lemon towered over the two students, his academic gown billowing in the soft breeze, making him look like a giant bat. As he opened his mouth to speak, Ruby heard a 'ping' and the headmaster hurriedly took out his phone to read a text.

He smiled broadly, then looked at the two students and shrugged his shoulders.

'Ah, who cares?'

Ruby and Andre stared after the headmaster as he wandered off singing 'We're in the Money'.

CHAPTER
10.

The next morning as the girls were getting ready for school, Ruby heard an excited squeal from the other side of the dorm.

'Check this out!' said Fav pointing to her laptop. 'It's Rosemary Arrow's online article.'

The girls huddled around Fav so they could all read it. Ruby saw the headline, 'Dynamic Duo!' and underneath was a photo of her and Andre.

'Oooh — they look so cute together,' said Fav with a grin.

Ruby went bright red and felt Sasha's eyes boring into the back of her head.

She noticed at the bottom of the article there were video links to her and Andre's goals. There was also another link with the heading: 'Andre and Ruby weren't the only ones on target!' Fav clicked on the third link and up came the drone footage of Sasha being covered by a giant mass of pelican poo. A loud 'splat' sound effect had been added, making the incident look even funnier.

Ruby peeked over her shoulder and could see that Sasha was about to explode. The tall bully moved towards her, but stopped when she spotted the pen in Ruby's hand. Without saying a word, Sasha stomped out of the dorm, as Ruby gripped her pen and smiled.

After school that afternoon, Ruby went to the art room to catch up with Andre.

The art room had tall floor-to-ceiling windows that let in the sunshine and provided a lovely view of the multi-coloured flowerbeds outside. Square benches that seated four students each were haphazardly spread throughout the room, and along one of the walls were built-in shelves housing neatly sorted sheets of cardboard, pencils, paints, crayons, glue, strands of wool, beads and any other bits and pieces needed to create a work of art. It was Ruby's favourite place on the school's grounds.

'Hope you're happy to meet here,' said Andre with a grin as she walked in. 'Miss Atkinson said we could use it whenever we want to work on the magazine.'

'Cool,' said Ruby.

Andre pulled out two chairs at one of benches, and they sat down facing each other near the front of the class. He pointed to the whiteboard where he had written:

Things to discuss with Ruby:
Aim of magazine?
Articles?
Drawings?
Timeline?
What help do we need?

'I made that stupid list, then I thought, why don't we start off by just talking? You know, find out a bit more about each other.'

'Great,' said Ruby. 'I hate lists!'

'Good to know … I'll add that to my list,' said Andre.

Ruby smiled. 'What else would you like to know?'

'Okay, how did you get into drawing?' asked Andre.

'My dad,' replied Ruby. 'He was an artist, and I used to watch him paint when I was little …'

Ruby stopped talking, and after an uncomfortable pause tried to switch the conversation to Andre.

'What about your parents?' she asked. 'Are they both professional soccer players?'

'Ha! No, Dad's a chef. He's runs a Japanese restaurant and also an Italian one — he's Japanese–Italian.'

'Wow. And your mum?'

'She's a lawyer — she's always flying somewhere for some pretty cool cases.'

'A chef and a lawyer — that's the perfect relationship,' said Ruby.

'How come?'

'If your dad accidentally poisons someone, your mum can defend him!'

Andre burst out laughing and Ruby smiled again. Her shoulders dropped and she leaned back in her chair.

'The worst thing about having a lawyer as your mum, is you never win any arguments,' said Andre. 'At least your dad can help you with your drawings ...'

Ruby looked down and clasped her hands together.

'You okay?' asked Andre softly. 'I didn't mean to upset you.'

Andre leaned forward with a concerned look on his face, and waited until Ruby was composed enough to speak.

'My dad ... he ... passed away four years ago.'

'I am *so* sorry ... I had no idea ... you must really miss him.'

'Yeah.'

'Don't tell me if you don't want to, but how did he …'

Ruby took a deep breath.

'He was painting on some rocks by the ocean … and a freak wave came in and …'

'Oh Rubes, that's terrible.'

Ruby looked up and nodded. She had never spoken to anyone about her father's death, and it felt nice to share her feelings.

'It must have been awful for your mum, too,' added Andre.

'Yeah, she … hasn't been the same since. The saddest thing is she started dating the worst … here I'll show you.'

Ruby pulled out the drawings of her mum's boyfriends and handed them to Andre.

'This is hilarious!' he said holding up Ruby's cartoon of 'Bad Breath Barry'. 'And "Dodgy Dave" looks like a shocker!'

'That's Mum's current boyfriend — he's the worst of a very bad bunch.'

'So, what do you do when you're feeling … down?' asked Andre.

'Draw. There's this fantastic spot behind the school I like to sneak off to.'

'Nice. It's great you've got your own special place.'

'Maybe not for much longer. I found a For Sale sign hidden in some bushes, and on the weekend, I saw Mr Lemon slapping a Sold sticker on it.'

'That land belongs to the school — well, it used to any-way,' explained Andre.

'What do they use it for?' asked Ruby.

'It's kind of like Hetherington Hall's outdoor classroom. Geography classes always go there for nature trips, and the school sometimes uses it for orienteering competitions. Oh, and Mr Chol and Miss Atkinson take students there for an amazing ghost tour on Halloween night — everyone loves it.'

'Cool! But if the school wanted to sell the land, why hide the For Sale sign? Why not put up a giant billboard next to the road so that everyone could see it?'

'Something strange is going on,' said Andre, 'And obviously Mr Lemon is involved.'

'Well, he was whistling, and that's not normal,' said Ruby.

'And how weird was he in the corridor yesterday?'

They both started singing 'We're in the Money', and laughed.

'Wish we knew what he was up to,' said Ruby.

'I might have a way to find out. Follow me!'

But Ruby didn't have time to ask any questions. Andre was already heading towards the door. She followed him out of the art room, and then to a storeroom off the main corridor in the administration building.

Andre looked around cautiously to make sure the coast was clear, then opened the door and gestured for Ruby to go inside. Andre followed. The storeroom looked as if it should have been called the 'junk room'. Paint was peeling from the walls and there were large boxes spread out on the floor, some full, some empty. There was also a bank of shelves filled with a random assortment of objects, from rolled up maps to mouldy hockey goalie pads.

Andre pointed at the roof, then nimbly scaled the shelves and pushed open a trapdoor that led into the ceiling.

Ruby whispered, 'Aha!' and quickly climbed up after him. Once inside the roof, she discovered it was dark and extremely dusty.

'Someone should do a spring-clean up here!' she whispered.

Andre turned and smiled, 'Make sure you stay on the beam.'

'How come?'

'So you don't fall through the ceiling!'

'Thanks! Anything else I should know?'

'Watch out for possum droppings!'

'Great!'

Andre began crawling into the darkness, and Ruby stuck close behind him. After about a minute, he raised his hand to signal for her to stop, and pointed at a vent on his right.

'That's Mr Lemon's office down there,' he whispered. 'He always has his phone on loudspeaker, so you can hear what he's saying.'

They lay down along the beam so they could see into the headmaster's office through the vent. Mr Lemon was sitting at his desk and appeared to be picking his nose. *Gross!* A minute later his phone started ringing and he pushed a button, then leaned back on his chair.

'Headmaster Lemon speaking.'

'Oliver, how are you?'

Ruby's ears pricked up. *I know that voice!*

'Couldn't be better, Dave …'

'It's my mum's boyfriend,' whispered Ruby. 'Dodgy Dave!'

Even in the darkness Ruby could tell Andre looked surprised.

'Everything went to plan,' continued Mr Lemon. 'It was *so* easy to convince the school board to sell that useless piece of land, and as I was in charge of the sale, I made sure no one else knew about it.'

'Genius,' said Dodgy Dave. 'And when no one offered to buy the land …'

'… I generously told the school I'd buy it myself, at a very *reasonable* price.'

'A reasonable price for land you're not allowed to build anything on,' said Dodgy Dave with a chuckle.

'Speaking of which, how did you go with the council?'

'All good,' said Dodgy Dave. 'I've paid off the mayor and three of the councillors. At the next council meeting they'll vote to have that land re-zoned for commercial use.'

'So when can I start chopping down all the trees?' asked the headmaster.

'You'll be able to start building your Lemonsville Theme Park within …'

Ruby's nose began to itch in reaction to all the dust that had collected in the ceiling. *Please don't sneeze! Please don't sneeze! Please don't—*

'A-a-a-choooooo!'

Mr Lemon's eyes shot up to the ceiling.

'I'll call you back, Dave!' he said cutting off the conversation. The headmaster rushed to the window and called out to the groundsman who was raking up some leaves nearby.

'Gus! Someone's in the roof — seal off all the exits and trap them!'

'Easy. There's only one way in or out of that roof, and that's through the storeroom …'

Ruby's heart pounded as she watched Mr Lemon race out of the room.

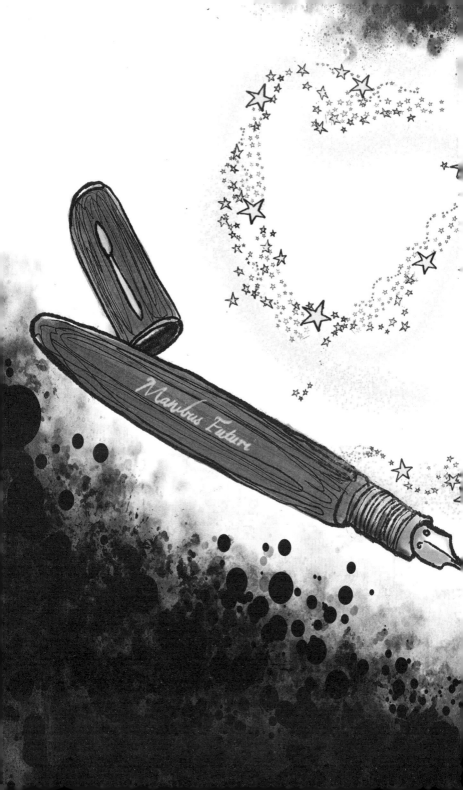

CHAPTER

Ruby and Andre frantically started crawling towards the trapdoor.

There were other vents positioned alongside the beam, and through one Ruby caught a glimpse of the headmaster striding along the corridor, his academic gown fluttering behind him. As she scuttled forward, she glanced down at the next vent and was relieved to see Mr Lemon had been held up by Miss Luxton.

'Headmaster, I think the school should provide two female soccer scholarships— '

'Not now, Miss Luxton!'

'But I have this proposal—'

'Email it to me!'

'I did two weeks ago, and you never responded ...'

'Email it again!'

They were only ten metres from the trapdoor but Ruby

knew Mr Lemon was on the move again, as she saw him flash past through the nearest vent. *We're not going to make it!*

Suddenly there was a crashing sound below them.

'Look where you're going!' screamed the headmaster.

'Look where *I'm* going? You ran into *me*,' said Mr Chol.

Ruby could see the headmaster sitting on his backside, with Mr Chol and Miss Atkinson standing over him. Mr Chol was holding an empty coffee mug, and Mr Lemon's crisp white shirt was covered in brown liquid.

'That's a nasty stain,' said Miss Atkinson, trying not to laugh.

Ruby climbed through the trapdoor into the storeroom and scrambled down the shelves, closely followed by Andre. With Mr Lemon only metres away, there was no escape. She scanned the room and spotted a big empty cardboard box in the corner. The two of them jumped inside and hurriedly pulled down the flaps to hide themselves.

Seconds later the door burst open and Mr Lemon entered, followed by Gus the groundsman, who was carrying a small ladder. Ruby held her breath and peered through a crack in the corner of the box. She watched Gus set up the ladder underneath the trapdoor and step back so that Mr Lemon could climb it.

'I'm not going up there!' said Mr Lemon.

'Why not?'

'I don't want to get dirty.'

The groundsman stared at the headmaster's coffee-stained shirt and muttered, 'Bit late for that.' He then hopped onto the first rung and headed towards the ceiling.

After Gus disappeared into the roof, Ruby looked over at Mr Lemon, but immediately turned away in disgust. *OMG! He's picking his nose again!*

A few minutes later, the groundsman's feet appeared back on the ladder.

'I think I found your intruder,' he announced. He spun around on the ladder and held up a small possum.

'Here's your spy!'

Mr Lemon let out a giant sigh of relief.

'Ha! Ugly little critter, isn't he?'

The possum started wriggling frantically, eventually freeing itself from Gus' clutches. It then leapt onto Mr Lemon's face and began clawing at his forehead.

'Get it off me! Get it off me!' shrieked the headmaster as he fell to the ground.

Ruby let out a tiny snort, but fortunately the sound was drowned out by the groundsman's howling laughter.

Eventually Gus pulled the possum off Mr Lemon's balding head, which was now covered with tiny scratch marks.

'Get rid of that thing,' hissed the headmaster.

'Aww, how about I put this cute little fella in the forest behind the school?'

'Perfect,' sneered Mr Lemon.

Ruby and Andre stayed hidden for several minutes after the two men had left, before emerging from the large brown box.

'Somehow we have to stop that theme park,' said Andre. 'All that beautiful forest being destroyed just so Mr Lemon gets rich — it's not right.'

'Maybe we could write about it in the school magazine?' suggested Ruby.

'Yes! That's a great way to let everyone know what's really going on.'

Ruby's smile suddenly turned into a frown.

'Although … won't Mr Lemon check everything before it gets printed?'

'Maybe I can fix that,' said Andre. 'But now we're going to need some help to get all the other articles done.'

'How about I talk to Fav and Dougal?'

'Cool. Let's all meet tomorrow after school in the art room.'

Ruby smiled. For the first time in years, she felt like she had a purpose.

Ruby was busting to go to the toilet when she arrived back at the boarding house, so she headed to the large red-and-white-tiled bathroom on the second floor. She walked down to the toilet on the end, and as she was shutting the door she heard a familiar voice.

'Check to make sure no one's here,' ordered Sasha.

Instinctively, Ruby jumped up onto the toilet so that her feet could not be seen.

'All clear,' said Miranda crouching down on her knees.

'Did you check properly?'

'What? Do you think I'm stupid?'

During the awkward silence that followed Miranda's question, Ruby stepped down from the toilet and cautiously peeked around the cubicle door.

'As I was saying, I can't do anything to Poo-by because of that dumb pen,' complained Sasha.

'You'll have to wait until she runs out of ink,' suggested Miranda.

'Way ahead of you … check this out!'

Sasha pulled Ruby's bottle of ink out of her pocket and unscrewed the lid.

'Bye, bye ink!' she announced.

Ruby winced as Sasha gleefully tipped the entire contents of the bottle down one of the bathroom basins. Sasha held up the empty bottle triumphantly, but her smug look quickly disappeared as the bottle refilled itself with ink.

Miranda looked stunned and took a step back.

'What the …?'

Sasha tipped out the ink again. And again. And again. But the same thing happened each time.

'Wh-wh-what are you going to do?' asked Miranda.

'Um, I'll … smash it!'

Sasha hurled the bottle at the bathroom wall, but instead of the sound of breaking glass, there was a dull thud.

The bottle seemed to flatten and stick to the wall, as if it was made of plasticine. It slowly slid downwards then reverted to its original shape when it touched the floor.

Sasha picked it up and threw it at the floor. This time the bottle bounced back like a rubber ball, hitting her in the face. She swore loudly and Ruby had to put her hand over her mouth to stifle a laugh.

Sasha nervously picked up the bottle and bolted out of the bathroom, with Miranda hot on her heels.

Five minutes later, Ruby strolled into the dorm and spotted Sasha with an ice pack on her face. The magical bottle of ink was now back on her desk, right where Ruby had left it. She flashed Sasha a confident smile, sat down in her chair and opened up her laptop. There was an email from her mother, and she let out a small sigh as she clicked on it.

Hey Rubes,
Great news! Dave's big deal has come off — not sure
where he's going to take us, but I overhead him talking
about theme parks!
Hope you're having fun — miss you!
Love Mum xx

Ruby clenched her fists and immediately started bashing out
her response.

Hi Mum,
All good here 2. I've started working on the school maga-
zine and we're going 2 expose Dodgy Dave & Mr Lemon
which will b gr8!
Have 2 go 2 dinner now — they r serving a casserole
that's reheated leftovers from 3 days ago. Yummy!
Take that holiday with Dave on your own — I couldn't
care less.
Love Rubes x

She thought about pushing send, but took a deep breath and
decided to delete a few words first.

Hi Mum,

All good here 2. I've started working on the school maga-
zine which will b gr8.

Have 2 go 2 dinner now — they are serving a casserole.
Yummy!

Take care,

Love Rubes x

She shook her head and sent the email before heading to the
dining room. *Casserole — bleurgh!*

The next afternoon, Ruby, Fav and Dougal sat around a
bench as they waited anxiously in the art room. Andre had
left to talk to the headmaster half an hour earlier, although
it seemed like much longer. His goal was to find out if Mr
Lemon would be checking the magazine closely before allow-
ing it to be published.

'Andre said Mr Lemon usually inspects every word
because he loves finding spelling mistakes,' said Ruby. 'So
let's not get our hopes up.'

The door opened slowly and Ruby watched Andre enter
with a sad look on his face.

'H-how did it go?' she asked.

'Really ...'

All of a sudden Andre smiled.

'… great!'

'You nearly gave us a heart attack!' said Dougal. 'What happened?'

'I said we knew he was incredibly busy and didn't want to bother him all the time about what was being included in the magazine.'

'And what did he say?' asked Fav.

'Luckily his phone started ringing, and I think he just wanted to get rid of me, so he said, "Whatevs. I don't care what's in it, just don't go over budget!"'

'So he won't know what's in the magazine until it comes out?' asked Ruby.

'Yep!' said Andre.

Everyone clapped and high-fived each other.

'So, what does everyone want to work on?' asked Andre.

'I could do the sports reports,' said Dougal. 'They're usually *really* boring, so could I add a few jokes?'

'Definitely!' said Andre. 'How about you, Fav?'

'I can write the club reports, like debating and chess, and I'll make sure they're more exciting than the normal ones, too.'

'Fantastic, Fav. Ruby?'

'I want to write about Mr Lemon's plans to ruin the forest, and also draw some cartoons of the teachers.'

'Excellent, Rubes,' said Andre. 'And I'll help with the editing on all of the articles, sourcing photos and doing the type-setting. Is everyone cool with that?'

'Yes!'

The school magazine meetings took place three times a week, and along with her visits to see Chirpy, they were the highlight of Ruby's time at Hetherington Hall.

It quickly became a tradition for Dougal to kick off the meetings with a joke. And it didn't matter how bad it was, his delivery always cracked everyone up. He would start laughing uncontrollably halfway through telling his gag, which would then set off his three friends. It created a lot of positive energy and brought them all closer together.

Ruby admired Fav's contribution to their little team. She was so smart that whenever she spoke, her friends would stop what they were doing and listen intently.

Ruby also appreciated the fantastic job Andre did as the magazine's editor. He was always supportive and built up everyone's confidence. A couple of times she caught him staring at her, then he would look away and smile. She would smile too and then hastily re-focus on her drawings.

As the weeks sped by, Ruby realized she was enjoying her

new school. She still had to put up with Miss Luxton and Miss Vermin, but no longer had to worry about Sasha, who had suddenly stopped calling her Poo-by. As the mid-term break approached, Ruby even sent her mum an email without being prompted.

Hey Mum,
Just checking in 2 c how u r. Fav, Dougal, Andre & I r
working hard 2 finish the school magazine — still have a
few drawings 2 do.
Look forward 2 c-ing u 2morrow night,
Love Rubes x

Ruby pushed send, then snuck off to the forest, as it was her last chance to see Chirpy before the break.

As she entered the scrub, she spotted a giant new sign that said, 'Coming Soon — Lemonsville Theme Park!' It included a photo of Mr Lemon giving a cheesy thumbs-up.

Ruby stared in disbelief. *Of all the models he could have used … he chose himself!*

She walked on, admiring the beauty of her surroundings and breathing in the fresh clean air. When she arrived at the clearing, there was no sign of Chirpy, so she cleared her throat and started making bird noises.

'Chirp chirp. Chirp chirp. Chirp chirp.'

A flash of colour to her left announced her friend's arrival.

'Hey, Chirpy!'

The bird cocked its head and started chirping back.

Ruby sat down on the flat rock, pulled out her pad and immediately came up with an idea for a drawing. She sketched Chirpy wearing a shower cap in an old-fashioned bathtub, with lots of soap suds and a small rubber duck. Underneath the drawing she wrote, 'Bird Bath!'

She held it to show Chirpy and said, 'You are *so* going to miss me when I'm gone.'

The bird chirped loudly.

'Yes you will!'

Ruby stared at the handsome bird and smiled.

'Look after yourself while I'm away, okay?'

Her little friend jumped up and down and started walking around in circles.

'Yes, I'll look after myself too … although who knows what'll happen after the school magazine comes out tomorrow.'

The next day after school, Ruby and her friends huddled around Andre's laptop at a tall bench in the art room.

'Let's take one last look,' suggested Andre.

First, they read through Fav's beautifully written club reports. *Wow!* thought Ruby. *She's even made chess sound exciting.*

Andre then scrolled down so they could read Dougal's sports articles. They were informative but also hilarious.

'Hey, can we look at Ruby's drawings again?' asked Dougal. Andre went through each of them, including the ones of Mr Lemon and Miss Vermin. Everyone burst out laughing.

'But this one is my absolute favourite,' said Andre, clicking on Ruby's cartoon of Miss Luxton. The boarding house mistress had a soccer ball for a head, with a thought bubble coming out from the soccer ball, which was thinking about more soccer balls. The caption at the bottom read: 'Who says I'm a soccer head?'

'It's funny because it's true,' laughed Dougal.

Ruby's article about Mr Lemon's plans for the land behind the school was the last one they looked at. It concluded with the rallying statement: 'The world needs more trees, not more theme parks!'

Andre, Fav and Dougal all gave Ruby a round of applause.

'Aww, shucks!' she said.

After a moment of silence, Ruby looked over at everyone's packed bags by the door.

'Ready for the emergency exit?' she asked.

The four students nodded, piled their hands one on top of each other's, and then pressed send together.

Instantly the school magazine was on its way to all of the Hetherington Hall students, parents, teachers and … its headmaster.

'Let's get out of here!' said Ruby.

CHAPTER 12

As the plane touched down, Ruby felt excited about seeing her mother. Her secret hope was for them to become much closer over the break.

She followed the long line of people off the plane and into the busy airport gate lounge, where she looked around expectantly. But instead of spotting her mum, she saw a tall man in a black suit and cap holding up a sign with her name on it.

Ruby's face dropped. She shook her head as the unsmiling chauffeur took her bags and led her to his car. She then spent the entire trip staring out the window and grinding her teeth.

When she arrived home, Adelaide bounded into the hallway and gave her a hug.

'Sorry we couldn't pick you up, sweetheart. Dave got a last-minute business call and there wasn't time for me to catch the train.'

'That's okay,' said Ruby without making any effort to return her mother's embrace.

Dodgy Dave stomped out of his study to join them. There were beads of sweat on his forehead and he flashed an insincere smile.

'Honey, why don't you make Ruby a hot chocolate, while I help her with her bags?' he said.

'Great idea! Can't wait to hear all your school stories, Rubes!'

As soon as Adelaide disappeared through the kitchen door, Dodgy Dave's face soured.

'What have you done?' he demanded.

Ruby shrugged her shoulders and looked at him blankly.

'Drop the innocent act! Your headmaster just told me about your stupid school magazine ...'

'It's actually an e-magazine ...' interrupted Ruby.

'I don't care if it was sent out by courier pigeons!' hissed Dodgy Dave. 'Thanks to your article, a journalist from the local paper has been asking some very awkward questions.'

Ruby tried to keep a straight face, but failed.

'Wipe off that grin, Missy, because if this theme park deal gets ruined, you and your mum will be living on the streets!'

Dodgy Dave stormed back to his study, leaving Ruby staring after him.

Busted

'So you're not going to help with the bags?' she asked under her breath.

Ruby calmly headed to her bedroom and retrieved the pen from her suitcase. As she walked towards her desk a strong surge of energy flowed into her body, but it felt different. This time she was *totally* in control.

'Nobody stands in my way,' she whispered as she pulled a piece of paper from the top drawer. Ruby sketched Dodgy Dave with bundles of money stuffed in his pockets, being arrested by the police, and added the word 'Busted!' underneath it. She leaned back in her chair and inspected her drawing with a cold smile.

Moments later, there was a loud knock at the door and Ruby rushed out of her bedroom.

'I'll get it!' yelled Dodgy Dave.

Ruby watched him open the door and take a step back when he saw two stern police officers standing in front of him.

'I'm Inspector Rod Vance and this is Senior Sergeant

Anita Lim. We wanted to talk to a …'

The inspector referred to a small pad he was holding.

'… Mr David Sykes.'

'Um, that's me,' said Dodgy Dave. 'But if this is about bribing councils … it's their word against mine!'

'Bribery? What are you talking about?' asked Senior Sergeant Lim.

'Nothing!'

'We're here about an alleged counterfeit operation,' said Inspector Vance.

'Counterfeit? Ha! You've definitely got the wrong guy!'

Right at that moment, a one-hundred-dollar note fell out of Dodgy Dave's sleeve.

Senior Sergeant Lim stooped down and picked it up. After inspecting it closely, she gave Inspector Vance a knowing nod, and said, 'Mr Sykes, can you please empty your pockets?'

'S-s-ure.' Dodgy Dave nervously reached into his pockets and pulled out wad after wad of one-hundred-dollar notes.

'B-b-but, this isn't mine!'

'We hear that a lot, sir,' said Inspector Vance.

Senior Sergeant Lim shook her head in disgust. 'The ink's not even dry.'

'Mr Sykes, would you mind accompanying us to the station?' asked the inspector.

As the police car drove away, Ruby beamed with satisfaction. *Good riddance to bad rubbish!* she thought, remembering one of Bertie's favourite sayings.

She strode towards the kitchen feeling confident that, at last, she could start to repair the fractured relationship with her mother. But when she poked her head through the door, Adelaide's face was buried in her hands, and she was sobbing uncontrollably. Ruby was shocked, and looked warily at the pen as she pulled it from her pocket. *What have I done?* she thought.

She rushed over to comfort her distraught mother, but stopped halfway when an overwhelming burst of energy sprang from the pen.

Instead of hugging her mum, Ruby smiled, turned around and skipped back to her bedroom.

As the taxi dropped Ruby in front of the boarding house four days later, she let out a sigh of relief. It had been the worst mid-term break ever! Her mum had rarely left her bedroom, and when she did she was on the phone to Dodgy Dave or his lawyer. They had eaten meals together, but Adelaide had hardly spoken a word.

In one of their few conversations, Ruby had halfheartedly offered to stay with her mother instead of returning to Hetherington Hall.

'Thanks, sweetheart,' replied Adelaide. 'But Dave's paid your fees for the whole term, as well as a non-refundable return flight, so you'd better head back to school.'

As Ruby lugged her bags up to the dorm, the thought of catching up with Fav, Dougal and Andre cheered her up.

But her smile quickly disappeared when she entered the room. The other girls stared at Ruby in silence, and Miss Atkinson was sitting at her desk, wringing her hands.

'What's going on?' asked Ruby, putting down her bags.

'Miss Luxton has asked me to take you to see the headmaster,' said Miss Atkinson softly.

Ruby's heart was pounding as she followed her art teacher out of the boarding house. As they walked past the three-tiered fountain, Miss Atkinson suddenly stopped and put her hand on Ruby's shoulder.

'Mr Lemon is on the war path about the school magazine, but Mr Chol and I think you all did a fantastic job.'

'Thanks,' mumbled Ruby.

When they arrived at Mr Lemon's office, Miss Atkinson knocked on the door. After a lengthy wait it was opened by a grumpy-faced Miss Luxton, who beckoned Ruby to come inside. Miss Atkinson tried to follow, but her path was blocked by the boarding house mistress.

'And where do you think you're going?'

'I'm here to support Ruby,' said Miss Atkinson.

'Don't worry, I'll make sure she receives all the support she *deserves*.'

'But—'

'No buts!' yelled Miss Luxton, slamming the door and herding Ruby into the middle of the room.

Mr Lemon was seated behind his impressive mahogany desk, with Miss Vermin standing next to him. Miss Luxton went and stood on the other side of the headmaster and folded her arms. Then all three of them stared at Ruby in silence, with competing scowls on their faces.

Ruby swallowed nervously, shut her eyes and thought about her dad. Whenever she was upset or in trouble, he had always known what to say to make her feel better. She remembered a time when she had carelessly knocked a bowl of cereal onto the kitchen floor. There was mess everywhere, and tears had quickly formed in her eyes because she felt terrible about what she had done. But Bertie had simply given her a wink and said, 'Hey, no use crying over spilt milk!'

Her thoughts about her father were broken by a loud knock at the door, and she turned to see Andre enter, followed closely by Mr Chol.

'What are you doing here Marley?' asked Mr Lemon.

'I'm here to support Andre …'

'There's no need for that, so goodbye.'

Mr Chol looked unimpressed but held his tongue and quietly left the room.

Andre walked over, flashing Ruby a confident grin, and she smiled back.

'There's nothing to be happy about, Miss West,' growled Mr Lemon as he held up a printout of the magazine. 'You are in *big* trouble.'

'Yes,' said Miss Vermin. 'How dare you draw mean cartoons of the teachers? As a totally random example …'

She angrily held up Ruby's drawing of her.

'… in this one, you made me look like I wear too much make-up.'

Mr Lemon and Miss Luxton looked at each other and raised their eyebrows.

'It's a form of bullying,' continued Miss Vermin, 'and, as you know, I can't stand bullying!'

Ruby turned to look at Andre and they both rolled their eyes.

'And what about *my* cartoon?' said Miss Luxton. 'I don't even get it. What's with all the soccer balls?'

This time Mr Lemon and Miss Vermin exchanged glances.

'And as for mine,' said the headmaster, 'You made me look like an old man ... and I'm only in my early forties.'

Miss Vermin looked at Miss Luxton and mouthed, 'Early forties?' Miss Luxton shook her head doubtfully.

'Miss West, putting the drawings aside for one moment,' continued Mr Lemon. 'I was particularly disappointed with your article about my plans to build the theme park.'

Ruby imagined how 'disappointed' all the beautiful trees were going to feel, after being flattened by a bulldozer.

'Your article made me sound like a money grubbing, heartless, environmental vandal, and as a result I've had angry calls from parents, local residents and a very nosy reporter called Rosemary Arrow. Look at this!'

The headmaster held up the *Hetherington Herald* from the previous day. It had his photo underneath a headline that said: 'Lemon Tries to Squeeze Juicy Deal!'

Ruby and Andre both looked at the floor to avoid laughing.

'That headline is *not* funny!' said the headmaster sternly.

'Oh, don't you get it?' asked Miss Luxton helpfully. 'Your surname's "Lemon", and you squeeze lemons, so ...'

'I get it!' roared the headmaster. 'It's just *not* funny!'

'No, not funny at all,' said Mrs Luxton obediently.

'Ruby, your article was totally misleading,' said Mr Lemon. 'And—'

'Sir, which part of Ruby's article was misleading?' interrupted Andre.

'Um, specifically? … Well, er, obviously the bit … where is it? …'

Mr Lemon started speed reading through the article to find an example, but soon gave up.

'It doesn't matter,' he said smugly. 'It's the cartoons that are the problem, because, as Miss Vermin says, they are a form of bullying. So Miss West, I have no choice … but to *expel* you.'

Ruby was too shocked to speak, but Andre immediately leapt to her defence.

'Mr Lemon, I'm the editor and *I* decided what went into the magazine, not Ruby. I take full responsibility—'

'Enough Mr Amano!' said the headmaster. 'Your editorial judgment was poor to include those cartoons, but Miss West drew them, so she's the one who must be punished.'

'But—'

'No buts!' said Miss Luxton.

'That's not fair …'

'My decision is final!' shouted Mr Lemon. 'Miss West, don't bother unpacking your bags, as you will be leaving Hetherington Hall first thing in the morning … for good!'

CHAPTER
13

Ruby sat on her bed spinning the pen between her fingers. She felt strangely numb. The decision to expel her had come as a complete shock, and the consequences were only just sinking in.

Eventually Fav broke the gloomy silence.

'I can't believe you're going, Rubes.'

'Well, at least someone's happy.'

They looked across at Sasha, who was grinning from ear to ear.

Ruby decided to draw something to wipe the smirk off her face, but was distracted when Miss Atkinson burst into the dorm.

'Ruby, you have a visitor in the common room!'

Ruby had no idea who it could be, so she hurried downstairs and peeked through the common room door. Sitting in the far corner was an immaculately dressed woman with beautifully coiffed hair and expensive-looking jewellery.

Ruby entered and nervously approached the intimidating-looking lady, who gave her a warm smile. The smile was strangely familiar.

'Hi, you must be Ruby. My name's Anne-Marie Amano — Andre's mother. He told me what happened, and I'd like to help.'

Ruby could hear Mr Lemon's annoying voice on the other side of the door.

'… so let's have a final farewell toast, to the pesky … Miss West!'

This was followed by laughter and the sound of clinking glasses.

Without knocking, Anne-Marie barged into the headmaster's office with Ruby right behind her. Mr Lemon, Miss Vermin and Miss Luxton froze like statues. They were wearing party hats and holding champagne glasses.

'Celebrating something?' said Anne-Marie.

'No, no … nothing at all,' said Mr Lemon, whipping off his colourful paper hat. 'So, um, how can I help you, Mrs Amano?'

'I'm here acting on behalf of my client, Ruby West, whose

attendance at this school has been invalidly terminated.'

Mr Lemon smoothed down what was left of his dark greasy hair, and puffed out his chest.

'Anne-Marie … may I call you Anne-Marie? I don't think we need to get all "legal" here,' he said. 'As headmaster I have absolute authority to expel any student, any time, for whatever reason I want …'

'Where in the school's charter does it say that?' interrupted Anne-Marie. She pulled a document from her briefcase and handed it to the stunned headmaster.

'Well … it may not say those *exact* words but, you know, reading between the lines …'

'Did you give any guidelines to the editor of the school magazine about what should or should not go into the publication?' demanded the lawyer.

'Well I, um …'

'Specifically, did you say to the aforementioned editor, "Whatevs. I don't care what's in it, just don't go over budget!"?'

'Um … that does sound *vaguely* familiar …'

'So *you* set no content restrictions *whatsoever*, and then expelled *my* client because some of her satirical cartoons were included?'

'Well, when you say it like *that*, it does sound a teensy bit harsh …'

'How will the school board feel when they hear *all* the facts?'

'There's really no need to trouble the board,' said the headmaster, who was now sweating profusely.

He looked at Ruby thoughtfully, then suddenly pointed at her and called out, 'Gotcha!'

Ruby screwed up her face in confusion.

'What do you mean, Mr Lemon?' demanded Anne-Marie as she folded her arms.

'Obviously I was totally kidding about expelling Ruby … it was all a prank! You know, to get her back for those, um, hilarious drawings.'

'Hilarious?' said Miss Vermin, her eyes nearly popping out of her head.

'Yes, the Miss Luxton cartoon was *really* funny,' said Mr Lemon 'And Ruby, you captured Miss Vermin perfectly with the make-up angle …'

Miss Vermin muttered under her breath, 'You have *got* to be kidding me!' as the headmaster continued.

'… and obviously you made me look much older for comedic purposes, yes?'

Ruby shook her head demonstrably.

'Well, I can forgive that,' said the headmaster with a fake smile. 'Let's just forget this whole thing *ever* happened …'

'We'll do no such thing!' snapped Anne-Marie.

She turned to Ruby and asked in a softer voice, 'How are you feeling?'

Ruby felt pretty awesome — she loved watching Mr Lemon squirm — but she replied, 'Hurt. Deeply hurt.'

'And do you feel the headmaster has ruined your reputation?'

Ruby nodded sorrowfully.

Anne-Marie shot the headmaster a look of such disgust that he took a step backwards in fright.

'Clearly my client has endured extensive pain and suffering as a result of your so-called "prank", said the feisty lawyer. 'And she will need to be compensated.'

'C-c-compensated?' stammered the headmaster.

'That's right! Pain and suffering does *not* come cheap.'

'Surely there's something we can do to fix up this little … misunderstanding.'

Anne-Marie put her hands on her hips and shook her head.

'I'll need to talk to my client,' she said.

Ruby followed Anne-Marie out of the room, and when they were out of earshot they both burst out laughing.

'You were *amazing*!' said Ruby.

'So were you! "Hurt. Deeply hurt"!'

They both laughed again.

'So Ruby, what would you like to come out of this?' asked Anne-Marie.

'For me, Andre, Fav and Dougal, it's all about stopping Mr Lemon from destroying the forest.'

Anne-Marie sighed and shook her head sadly.

'I've had a quick look into it, and unfortunately he isn't breaking the law. The school board approved his purchase of the land, and the council then made it available for commercial use. Even though the deal stinks, we can't prove anything.'

Ruby could not hide her disappointment, and it was her turn to sigh.

'Do you have *any* good news?' she asked.

'Well, we *could* make Mr Lemon go through a bit of embarrassment for trying to expel you, if that's something you—'

'Yes!'

A short time later Ruby and her lawyer re-entered the headmaster's office.

'Okay Mr Lemon,' said Anne-Marie. 'Here's what it will take to make this go away …'

The next morning the assembly hall was packed with students, as Mr Lemon walked onto the stage. He wore the expression of a boy in a dentist's waiting room who hadn't cleaned his teeth since the last visit. He placed a typed note on the lectern, fiddled with the knot of his tie, and then began to read his prepared statement.

'Students, before we start assembly, I would like to make an … er … official um … apology … to … Ruby West. I sort of … accidentally expelled her, for doing some drawings that are, um, very f-f-funny …'

Giant images of Ruby's cartoons of Miss Vermin, Miss Luxton and Mr Lemon suddenly appeared on the projector screen behind the headmaster. The students all laughed as Miss Vermin and Miss Luxton, who were seated on stage, blushed and looked at the floor.

'Come on, they're not *that* funny,' said Mr Lemon among the cackles.

'Yes they are!' called out Dougal, which set the students off laughing again.

The headmaster shook his head and ploughed on with his statement.

'I admit that I was … wr … wr … wrong, and I am very s-s-s … sorry for the trauma I caused Miss West and I ap-ap … apologize unreservedly for my actions.'

The students, with the exception of Sasha, jumped up and gave Ruby a standing ovation. Mr Chol and Miss Atkinson, who were seated together, exchanged a subtle fist pump.

Ruby blushed as she looked over at a smiling Andre, and then laughed when she saw Dougal doing a celebratory 'moon walk' dance move in the aisle.

When the clapping died down, Mr Lemon cleared his throat.

'Ahem. If Mr Marshman could return to his seat, we will move on with the rest of assembly.'

Dougal grinned before scampering back to his spot at the end of the row. The headmaster nodded then resumed speaking in a far more confident tone.

'I know there have been a few *minor* concerns about the construction of the Lemonsville Theme Park ...'

Ruby folded her arms and whispered to Fav, 'Yeah, none of us want it!'

'... but I'm pleased to announce today that once the park is completed, every Hetherington Hall student will get two free rides ... each term!'

Nearly every boy and girl in the assembly hall leapt to their feet and started cheering the headmaster.

'Okay, so maybe a few of us *do* want it,' muttered Ruby.

Back in the boarding house at lunchtime, Ruby was getting her books ready for the afternoon when Fav

yelled, 'Rubes, check this out.'

Ruby went over and found Fav reading an online article in the *Hetherington Herald*.

The heading said, 'Lemonsville — Creating Local Jobs for Local People!' and the author of the article was Oliver Lemon.

'He can't do that!' said Ruby.

'Unfortunately, he can,' said Fav. 'It's a paid ad made to look like a real news article.'

Ruby gritted her teeth and scanned the opening paragraph.

When I bought this land, the idea of building a theme park had not even entered my mind. But then I thought, 'What's something I could give the community that would benefit them forever …'

'I'm going to be sick!' said Ruby.

Fav glanced at the pen in Ruby's hand and frowned.

'What's the matter?'

'Your pen … since the break, you seem to be carrying it around all the time,' said Fav.

'I don't know about *all* the time,' said Ruby.

'You don't sleep with it, do you?'

Ruby didn't respond.

'OMG, you do!'

'Just to keep it safe!' said Ruby.

'Rubes, what's going on?'

'I don't know, Fav. It's weird. At the start the pen only worked when I was mad or scared, but now I can totally control it. Pretty cool, hey?'

Ruby stared at the pen in awe, without noticing that Fav had walked off without answering her question.

That afternoon, Miss Vermin was in a foul mood.

'You were all laughing in assembly this morning,' she said. 'But anyone who laughs in *this* class, won't be laughing.'

Fav's hand shot up in the air.

'Put your hand down, Faviola!' yelled the teacher. 'I know what I just said doesn't make sense, but you know what I mean!'

Ruby watched her friend roll her eyes, then heard someone say, 'Psst!'

She turned to her right and saw that Miranda was trying to get her attention.

'Those drawings in the magazine were like, *so* funny!'

Ruby could not hide her surprise.

'Really? I mean, thanks.'

Miss Vermin's harsh voice drew Ruby's attention back to the front of the class.

'As none of you have submitted your geography home-work, you will *all* have detention after school.'

'But it wasn't due until tomorrow,' said Fav.

'No, I distinctly remember saying it was due on the twenty-fourth,' said Miss Vermin.

'Yes ... and today is the twenty-third,' pointed out Dougal.

'Well I *meant* the twenty-third, so you all have detention!'

There was an eruption of groans, and Fav muttered, 'That is so unfair!'

'Right!' yelled Miss Vermin. 'Faviola, you will be in deten-tion for an *extra* half an hour! Anyone else want to say any-thing?'

An angry silence descended upon the classroom, and the teacher turned to write some questions on the whiteboard.

Ruby tightened the grip on her special pen, then calmly pulled out a piece of paper. She quickly sketched a cartoon of Miss Vermin doing a burp, with the caption, 'Excuse me!', then smiled as she sat back in her seat.

Less than a minute later, the teacher turned and spoke to the class.

'There are ten main types of clouds, but the ones we'll

focus on—' Miss Vermin suddenly burped so loudly the whiteboard started shaking.

'Um, excuse me that was—' Miss Vermin then let out an even bigger burp.

'Sorry about *(burp)* this *(burp)*. Don't *(burp)* worry about *(burp)* the *(burp)* detention *(burp) (burp) (burp)*...'

Miss Vermin rushed out the door with one final, massive burp.

Miranda leaned over and smiled when she saw Ruby's drawing.

'Cool!'

Ruby smiled back then glanced over at Fav and gave her a thumbs-up. But Fav gently shook her head and looked away. Ruby responded by folding her arms and poking out her tongue sarcastically.

CHAPTER
14

On Saturday morning before her soccer game, Ruby decided to do another drawing with her pen.

She remembered everyone laughing at her at training, and Fav and Dougal saying she was the worst player they had ever seen. *I'll show them!*

Ruby tapped the pen on her chin a couple of times, then did a quick cartoon of herself celebrating alongside two soccer balls in the back of the net. She thought about telling Fav, but her friend had been acting so strangely lately that she decided against it.

Just before the start of the game, Miss Luxton called in the players and pulled a piece of paper from her pocket.

'Okay, the starting eleven today are: Amelia, Michaela, Miranda, Afra, Georgina, Sasha, Faviola, Becky, Michiko, Charlotte, Mia and Ruby … Huh?'

Miss Luxton's eyes narrowed as she studied the piece of

paper again. She then looked up at Ruby and shook her head.

'Not sure what I was thinking, but don't let me down,' said the coach.

Ruby noticed Fav looking at her suspiciously, so she innocently shrugged her shoulders and ran onto the field.

Fav looked even more sceptical after Ruby kicked two goals … within the first two minutes! Those two, like her next six, were absolute flukes. The ball accidentally bounced off her feet, head, knees and even her back, before swerving through the air past the hapless goalkeeper.

After scoring her ninth goal, Miss Luxton called out, 'Congratulations, Ruby! You just broke Sasha's all-time school record!' Ruby grinned like a Cheshire cat and gave her coach a high-five as she ran past.

Moments later the siren sounded, and Ruby pumped her fist and hugged her nearest teammates.

'Whooo-hooo!' she yelled out.

As the team jogged towards the coach's box, Sasha looked across at Ruby and snarled, 'Cheat!'

Quick as a flash, Ruby pulled the pen out of her sock and pointed it at Sasha.

'What did you say?'

A look of horror appeared on Sasha's face and she immediately backed down.

'Nothing!'

Ruby smiled triumphantly, but stopped when she saw the disappointment on Fav's face.

'What's *your* problem?' she barked.

Fav did not respond. She simply turned her back, picked up her tracksuit and headed back to the boarding house.

Ruby always walked to school with Fav, but on the following Monday she watched her friend head off on her own.

Suit yourself! she thought.

Ruby was already in a bad mood because of an email that had arrived from her mother.

Hi Rubes,

Yes, I did get your email about sending fifty dollars for the school dance.

But unfortunately, because of Dave's problems with the police, they've frozen my bank account too, so I can't transfer any money.

Sorry!

Love Mum xx

Ruby rolled her eyes and typed back:

BUT I REALLY NEED IT!

She folded her arms impatiently and scowled for thirty seconds until she heard a 'ping'.

Rubes, I'm really, really sorry. Asked Dave to loan me the cash but he says he needs every cent for his upcoming court case. xx

Ruby picked up her pen and squeezed it, but this time its surge of power was devoid of any warmth. She put the pen down again, then angrily snatched up her books and stomped out of the boarding house.

Gossip about her magical drawings had spread throughout the school, and Ruby was quite happy about this development. This was because the bullies now feared her and the younger students treated her like a celebrity.

As she was walking past the administration building, a boy with a thick mop of blond hair ran up to her.

'Hey, you're Ruby aren't you?'

'Who's asking?'

'Jeremy Rundle.'

Ruby smiled. 'You're the kid who reckons he saw spiders coming out of Sasha's exploding pimple!'

'Spiders? No way … they were *scorpions*!'

Ruby rolled her eyes. 'What do you want?'

'I haven't done my maths homework, so could you please do a drawing that puts me in sick bay for a few hours?'

Ruby was about to say 'no' when Jeremy dropped to his knees and started begging.

'Pretty please?'

'Oh, all right!'

Ruby pulled out her pen and did a quick sketch of the boy with two tiny dots on his face.

'Done.'

'Thanks a million!' said Jeremy before running off.

As Ruby was walking back towards the boarding house for lunch, she spotted an ambulance parked in front of the administration building.

Two ambulance officers were wheeling a patient towards it, and Ruby squinted to try and see who was hurt. Her heart skipped a beat. *Jeremy Rundle!*

She rushed over and heard the ambulance officers talking.

'That's the most severe case of chicken pox I've ever seen. He won't be back at school for the rest of the term.'

As the trolley went by, Ruby noticed Jeremy's face was

covered with hundreds of spots. The boy looked at her and gave a thumbs-up.

'No school for the rest of the term! You're a legend, Ruby!' he whispered.

Ruby smiled back at him, as Fav walked over to see what was going on.

'What's up?'

'Another happy customer,' replied Ruby, holding up her pen.

They watched in silence as Jeremy was loaded into the ambulance.

After the doors were shut, one of the ambulance officers said to her colleague, 'That was touch and go — for a moment there, I thought we might lose him.'

A pang of guilt suddenly hit Ruby, as Fav gave her a horrified look.

'He could have died, Rubes,' said Fav.

'I was just trying to help!'

Ruby instinctively tightened her grip on the pen, and Fav shook her head.

'That pen has changed you ... and not in a good way.'

'That's not fair!' said Ruby defensively. 'Have you noticed how Sasha isn't bullying anyone any more?'

'You're right ... *Sasha* isn't.'

Fav started to walk away, but Ruby was determined to

have the last word.

'You're jealous!' she called out.

Fav held up her hand and kept walking.

Ruby frowned and gripped the pen even tighter. *What a loser!*

As Ruby lay in bed that night, her stomach felt as if it was twisted in knots. She could not understand why her best friend would tell her she had changed … for the worse! Suddenly the answer hit her like a ton of bricks: *because she is my best friend.*

Ruby thought about her recent soccer drawing, as well as using the pen to scare Sasha after the game, and nearly killing Jeremy Rundle with chicken pox. She felt her face turn bright red. She reached under her pillow, pulled out the pen and let out a sigh.

'From now on, I'll only use you for things that Fav would approve of,' she whispered.

The next morning Ruby wanted to tell Fav about her important decision, but her friend proved elusive and managed to avoid her all day. Finally, Ruby cornered her in the dorm after school.

'Hey Fav, why won't you even talk to me?'

'Mmm, probably because I'm *so* jealous.' Fav picked her toothbrush off her desk and headed for the door. 'Excuse me, I have to clean my teeth.'

Ruby rolled her eyes and started after her but was suddenly hit by a flash of anger. *Why is Fav being such a loser?*

She looked down and discovered the pen was in her hand. *Huh?*

Ruby could not remember picking it up. She took a deep breath, grabbed her sketchbook, and headed off to the forest. As she walked past the giant hedge and the old maintenance shed, Ruby's mind was racing with thoughts about Fav and her special pen. It felt as if her brain was being tugged and twisted in every direction.

But not long after squeezing through the fence, her thoughts were distracted by the rumbling sound of a large truck, and she quickly hid behind a nearby tree. Ruby watched as the truck screeched to a halt less than twenty metres away. It had a glossy red cabin with a sign on the door that said 'Lenny the Logger' with a drawing of a brawny lumberjack holding an axe. On the tray of the truck sat a faded yellow bulldozer.

A man in a blue singlet jumped out of the cabin, scratched his bottom, then lowered a ramp at the back of the truck. After leaping onto the tray, he hopped into the yellow earthmover, which started up with a powerful roar. He reversed it down the ramp with ease, before skilfully parking next to a cluster of trees. The man whistled as he got out of the bulldozer. Then he jumped back into the truck and hastily drove away.

Ruby's jaw tightened and she clenched her fists. She had considered leaving her pen behind to prove something to Fav but was now grateful she had brought it along. She raced over to the clearing, and quickly sketched a cartoon of the bulldozer being damaged by a variety of animals with sharp teeth. She sat back and admired her work. *That should make Fav happy.*

Chirpy flew in and landed a few feet from Ruby. The cute little bird jumped up and down, then ran around in circles. Ruby smiled and held up her drawing.

'This should make you happy too!' she said.

The next morning before school, Ruby found Fav at her desk reading an online article in the *Hetherington Herald*. She grinned when she saw the small headline: 'Bulldozer Destroyed by Wild Animals'.

'Fav, I know you don't like me using the pen, but thanks to one of my drawings, that bulldozer will be out of action forever.'

'I know.'

'Well, you don't look too happy ...'

Fav shook her head and scrolled up to the front page of the newspaper. The bolded headline screamed: 'Developers to Bring in the Big Guns!'

As Ruby read the article, her smile disappeared.

'After damage was sustained by a smaller bulldozer, the developer is replacing it with a much larger one. Nicknamed "The Terminator", this gigantic levelling machine will arrive on site in a few weeks' time. It is expected to complete the job five times quicker, but critics say it will cause considerably more environmental harm ...'

Ruby's heart sank.

'I've made things worse.'

'Yes, you have,' said Fav quietly.

Ruby slowly walked back to her desk, tossed the pen into her pencil case, and put her head in her hands. A feeling of self-loathing washed over her, but this was suddenly interrupted by Miranda, who was lurking awkwardly next to Ruby's cupboard.

'Hey Rubesmeister,' she said. *Rubesmeister?*

'Because we're kind of besties now, I have to tell you that Sasha took your ink bottle to the headmaster, so ...'

Ruby didn't wait for any more details from her new 'BFF'. She bolted out of the dorm and made a beeline for the storeroom in the administration building. When she got there, she looked around to make sure no one was in the corridor then quietly slipped inside. Without hesitating she scaled the shelves and pushed open the trapdoor.

When she arrived at the vent above Mr Lemon's office, she lay flat on her stomach and peered into the room below. She could see the headmaster talking on the phone, as Sasha sat patiently on the other side of his antique desk. Ruby cocked her ear to listen in.

'… just buy the cheaper material … it's easy for *you* to talk about safety, you're not the one paying for it … anyway, can't talk now, I've got someone with me.' Mr Lemon dismissively pushed a button to end the call, then looked at Sasha.

'Now, before we were interrupted, you said you had some important information.'

'Yes,' said Sasha gleefully. 'About Ruby West!'

Mr Lemon sat up in his chair. 'Go on,' he said, leaning forward.

'Once I tell you what she's been doing, you'll be able to expel her for sure.'

The headmaster leaned in closer and rubbed his hands together.

'Oooh, what did she do? Steal something? Graffiti school property … ?'

'No,' said Sasha dramatically. 'She's been using a magic pen.'

'Excellent! A magic pen. Well, she's in a lot of — what?'

'She's got this magic pen, and she used it to break my goal-scoring record …'

Mr Lemon slumped back into his chair.

'I thought you were smarter than this, Miss Sword.'

'No, wait, I can prove it!' said Sasha.

She pulled out the bottle of ink and held it up to show the headmaster.

'So what?'

'So … watch this!'

Ruby held her breath as Sasha walked over to the sink in Mr Lemon's office, then slowly tipped out the contents of the bottle. She pointed to the empty bottle jubilantly and said, 'See, it magically fills up … wait a minute.'

Sasha gave the empty bottle a shake. Nothing happened.

'Um, maybe it needs more time …'

'Grow up, Miss Sword!' snarled Mr Lemon as he stormed out of his office.

As soon as the door slammed shut, Ruby noticed the bottle had started to fill back up. Sasha stared at it in disgust.

'I hate you!' she hissed.

CHAPTER

15

It was Friday afternoon, a week before the school dance, and Ruby still had no money for a ticket. To make matters worse, her best friend was still avoiding her.

As she started walking back to the boarding house after school, Ruby spotted Fav in the distance and sprinted after her.

She eventually caught up at the far end of the Raleigh-Hinds oval, but Fav barely acknowledged her presence. After an awkward silence, Ruby said the first thing that popped into her head.

'I still can't afford to go to the dance — it's so unfair!'

It was only after she spoke that Ruby realized she was holding the pen. Fav noticed it too and frowned.

'Why don't you just draw yourself a fifty dollar note?' said Fav sarcastically.

Ruby gripped the pen tightly, and her eyes flashed with

anger. 'You know what,' she said, 'I will!'

She quickly drew a tree with a fifty dollar note as one of its leaves, and added the caption: 'Money *does* grow on trees!'

Ruby then ran over to the nearby Moreton Bay Fig and plucked out two fifty dollar notes that were caught in one of the branches. She waved them gleefully in the air and shouted, 'Hey, look-ee what I found! Now I can go to the dance — twice!'

Fav turned around to reveal her glasses were fogged up, and tears were streaming down her cheeks. She shook her head sadly before rushing off towards the boarding house.

Ruby felt like someone had kicked a soccer ball into her stomach; she could barely breathe. She looked down and stared at the pen. She used to feel safe and warm after using it; now all she felt was emptiness.

Instead of returning to the boarding house, Ruby walked out through the school gates, and headed into the town of Hetherington. She wanted to be on her own.

Usually when she felt sad, she wished her father was with her, but not now. *He would be so ashamed of me,* she thought. As she approached the strip of shops in the town's main street, she saw an old man sitting on the footpath. His clothes were tattered and he was seated next to an upturned hat with a sign that said, 'Need Money for Food'. Without thinking, she bent down and put the fifty dollar notes into the man's hat. He looked up and smiled as she walked off.

Ruby had a funny feeling she had seen him before, and then it struck her. His eyes looked just like … the man who had sold her the pen! She spun around, but the old beggar was already gone. *Just my imagination,* she thought, before turning and moving on.

Ruby soon found a spot out the front of a pharmacy, then pulled out her sketch pad and made a sign that said: 'Cartoon drawings ten dollars each!'

The street was busy and she promptly attracted a small line of customers. Her first drawing was for a mother who wanted a picture of her skateboarding son. Ruby sketched a cartoon of a boy wearing an astronaut's helmet, jumping over the moon on his skateboard. She added the caption, 'We have lift-off!'

'Perfect!' said the mother, handing over a ten dollar note.

An hour and a half later, Ruby had made the fifty dollars she needed, and a smile appeared on her face for the first time in weeks.

The following Friday evening, Ruby nervously entered the Hetherington Hall gymnasium and looked around.

A DJ was pumping out music in the corner, and along the far wall were linen-covered trestle tables laden with party pies, cakes and soft drinks. Above the basketball hoop Ruby spotted a large sign that said, 'School Dance'. *Just in case we weren't sure!*

She spotted Fav and gave her a wave, but her friend pretended not to see her and looked away. Ruby sighed and glanced towards the dancefloor. She laughed at the sight of Dougal, crouched down with his arms folded, doing a Russian Cossacks' dance, as a group of students stood around him and clapped. He gave Ruby a huge grin before breaking into an hilarious robot dance routine.

'You got da moves!' she called out.

Suddenly she felt a tap on her shoulder, and a voice from behind her said, 'Hey, Rubes.' She smiled and spun around.

'Andre!'

For the rest of the evening Ruby and Andre were inseparable. They talked together, danced together, ate together, then danced together some more. *This is the best night ever*, thought Ruby. She looked over at Fav, but she was still ignoring her. *Well, maybe not the best night ever.*

After the DJ played the last song of the evening, Ruby and Andre were walking off the dancefloor when Sasha 'accidentally' bumped into them.

'You two seem to be getting on well,' she said. 'I suppose you drew a happy little cartoon to make that happen, Ruby?'

'I didn't!' said Ruby.

'Yeah, just like you didn't draw a picture to help you kick nine goals in a game!'

'I … that was um, different …'

'*Sure* it was!' said Sasha as she walked off.

'Andre, I promise …'

Ruby looked into Andre's eyes and could see he was uncertain.

'I um, have to go,' he said. 'Mr Chol is taking us for an early run in the morning because we don't have a game tomorrow.'

'Okay,' said Ruby, trying to hide her disappointment.

She watched Andre disappear out the gymnasium door, then noticed Fav sitting on her own near the soft drinks table. Ruby walked over and pointed to the empty chair next to her.

'Is this seat taken?'

'I'm sorry, you'll have to join the queue with all the other people who can't wait to talk to me.'

The two girls smiled at each other and Ruby sat down.

'Fav, I'm sorry for being a total diva and a terrible friend,' said Ruby. 'I really screwed up.'

'You weren't a *total* diva,' said Fav. 'You were ninety-five per cent diva, tops!'

'Thanks!' said Ruby. She took a deep breath before continuing.

'It's weird, the pen … I thought I could control it, but … I've seen what it did to our friendship and I saw the way Andre looked at me tonight and … I won't be using it again.'

'Really?'

'I weighed up using it one last time to save the forest, but figured it'd probably just end up making things worse.'

'And we don't want "diva Ruby" to reappear!' added Fav.

'So, we agree … no more pen?' said Ruby.

'Agreed,' said Fav.

They shook hands and then hugged.

'Let's go back to the boarding house,' said Ruby.

When they arrived back at the dorm, Ruby tossed the pen onto her desk, grabbed her toiletries bag and headed off to the bathroom with Fav. As they cleaned their teeth they looked at each other in the mirror and burst out laughing. White foam sprayed everywhere and that made them laugh even harder.

'I've missed you,' said Ruby.

'Me too,' said her best friend.

They walked back into the dorm and Ruby headed for her bed, but her path was blocked by a smirking Sasha.

'Look what I've got!' she gloated, holding up Ruby's pen in

one hand and her bottle of ink in the other. Miranda walked in at that moment and her eyes lit up.

'Oooh Sasha! Can you feel its power?' she asked.

Sasha clasped the pen tightly and shut her eyes. After a few seconds she suddenly opened them.

'Nuh. Not a thing.'

'I wouldn't use that if I were you,' warned Ruby. 'It's dangerous.'

'Of course you'd say that, *Poo-by*.'

Ruby shook her head. *We're back to Poo-by again!*

Sasha went to her desk, took the lid off the ink bottle and attempted to fill the pen. As she flicked out the golden lever, dark blue ink went all over her top.

'Noooooooo! That's a brand new Dolce & Gabbana!'

'I told you it was dangerous,' said Ruby with a wry smile.

Sasha scowled, took out a piece of paper then started scribbling madly.

After a minute she said, 'Ta-dah!' and proudly held up her sketch.

Miranda took the drawing and looked confused. She then turned it upside down, before Sasha snatched it back.

'It's a bee stinging Poo-by on the bum.'

'*That's* a bee? I mean, oh yeah, good one!'

'And I've put a clock with 8 a.m. on it in the background,

to make sure it happens on the way to school. I want *everyone* to be watching!'

Ruby left the boarding house the next morning, hoping the
pen wouldn't work for Sasha. But just in case, she stuffed her
sketch pad down the back of her undies to protect her bottom.

According to her watch it was 7.59 a.m. and there were
no obvious signs of danger. Up ahead she spotted Gus the
groundsman standing on a ladder propped up against the
Moreton Bay Fig.

She gave him a wave, but as he waved back he suddenly
screamed and jumped to the ground.

'Bees!'

A giant swarm seemed to spring from nowhere and
zoomed directly at Ruby.

'Get her!' yelled Sasha, who was filming the attack on her
phone.

But the bees buzzed straight past Ruby and massed around
Sasha's head.

'Owwww! Get them off!' she screamed, before sprinting
away and diving into the fountain out the front of the boarding house.

As Ruby and Fav ran to help, Miss Luxton appeared and

bravely shouted, 'Stay back and let a teacher handle this.' Unfortunately, some of the bees then turned on her, and she fled back into the boarding house.

As a result of the commotion, nearly every student in the school rushed over to witness Sasha's embarrassing predicament. The bully now had her head underwater in the fountain, but that left her bottom exposed.

As the bees zeroed in on their target, Fav whispered to Ruby, 'Well, she did want everyone to watch!'

That night when Sasha entered the dorm, everyone went silent. She appeared to be wearing a giant padded nappy, her face was swollen, and her giant lips made it hard for her to talk.

'No-one ith to thay a wordth!' she announced.

OMG! She looks like a puffer fish! thought Ruby.

Sasha took out her 'bee' drawing and called Miranda over.

'I don't know whath wenth wrong,' she said.

'Mmm, maybe it was a bit hard to tell *that* was Ruby?' suggested Miranda, pointing at the picture.

'Are you kidding? I gave her a weally bad hair-thstyle, thereth no way that couldth be me!'

That night Ruby lay wide awake in bed. She was glad she no longer had her pen, and thrilled that she and Fav were besties again. *I may be pen-less, but at least I'm not friendless!*

Her mind turned once more to saving the forest, but she could not come up with a single idea that didn't involve using the pen.

Then Ruby suddenly smiled as a simple realization dawned on her: four heads are better than one. *Time to organize another meeting!* she thought, before falling sound asleep.

The next day after school, Ruby, Fav, Andre and Dougal met in the arts room.

'The reason for the catch-up is to try and come up with a plan to save the land,' announced Ruby.

After a thoughtful silence Dougal asked, 'Couldn't you just pull out "El Pen-o" and draw something to stop it?'

'I'm not using the pen any more,' explained Ruby. 'And Sasha has it anyway.'

Andre smiled on hearing this, then his face became serious. 'The problem is we're up against people who only care about money,' he said.

'But it's *so* beautiful over there,' said Ruby, taking out her sketch pad to show the others some of her drawings.

She started flicking through her illustrations when all of a sudden Fav said, 'What's that?'

'What's what?' asked Ruby.

Fav pointed to a drawing of a colourful bird. 'Rubes, did you copy that from a book?'

'No, that's Chirpy. Cute little thing always comes up to me when I'm drawing.'

'You're telling me *that* bird is in the forest next to the school?'

'Yup.'

'Incredible. They don't normally live around here,' said Fav. 'Ruby, that bird … is a Gouldian Finch!'

'I think I prefer the name Chirpy …'

'Don't you get it?'

'Clearly not …'

'It's an endangered bird! Mr Lemon can't clear that area if there's an endangered species in the habitat!'

CHAPTER

16

Ruby wrote the words 'Save Chirpy' on the whiteboard in the arts room, and turned to her friends.

'Andre, do you still have Rosemary Arrow's email address?'

'Yep.'

'Great. Let's send her a message explaining Chirpy's situation, and I've got some ideas for some cartoons we could attach.'

'Okay, while you're doing the drawings, we'll work on the email,' said Fav. 'Let's get this to Rosemary before dinner!'

Ruby sat down in the corner and immediately started sketching out her ideas. The cartoons didn't take long to produce because she was incredibly focused. *Can't let Chirpy down!* she thought as she worked.

'We're all done with the email, Rubes,' called out Fav half an hour later. 'Can we check out your drawings?'

'Sure,' said Ruby as she handed the first one to her friends.

It featured a giant black boot with the word 'Mayor' on it, preparing to stomp on a frightened little bird.

The caption read: 'Don't let council stand on Chirpy!'

'Fantastic!' said Dougal. 'Sad, but fantastic!'

'What's that line down the bottom?' asked Fav.

'It says #istandwithchirpy. I thought it might get people

talking about Chirpy on social media.'

'Great idea, Rubes,' said Andre. 'Maybe we could ask people to hang colourful scarves outside their homes, take photos and add the tag #istandwithchirpy?'

'Yeah that'd be cool,' said Dougal. 'What else do you have, Rubes?'

Ruby's second cartoon was a desolate drawing of chopped down trees and flattened bushes, and this time Chirpy was trembling behind a dead log.

At the top were the words, 'They want to build a haunted house …' and at the bottom it said '… but this is far more terrifying!'

'Amazing,' said Fav.

'I've got one more,' said Ruby.

She pulled out a drawing of a little boy at a theme park ticket booth.

The boy asks, 'How much?' and the shifty-looking man in the booth replies, 'Just the extinction of a species!'

'Love it!' said Andre.

'So which one should go with the email?' asked Ruby.

Her friends looked at each other and nodded.

'All three!' they said.

Fav then read out the moving email she, Andre and Dougal had written about the potential extinction of Chirpy's species, and it brought tears to Ruby's eyes.

'That's depressingly perfect,' she said.

The four friends once again stood over Andre's laptop and put their hands one on top of each other, so they could all press send together.

As the swooshing sound signalled the email was on its way to the *Hetherington Herald*, they all exchanged high-fives.

When Ruby walked into the dorm after dinner that evening, she felt tired but satisfied. She spotted Sasha and Miranda plotting away in the corner and rolled her eyes.

'Having fun?' she asked.

'Oh yeah,' said the still puffy-faced Sasha, holding up her latest drawing. Ruby squinted to try and work out what was on the paper.

'Um, is that a really short, two-legged giraffe?'

'It's you!' yelled Sasha. 'And guess what … you've got no hair!'

Miranda took the drawing and inspected it closely.

'Are you *sure* that looks like Ruby?'

Sasha snatched it back and wrote the word 'Ruby' next to an arrow that pointed at the girl's hairless head.

'Happy now?'

Miranda nodded and Sasha flashed an evil smile.

'Now all we have to do is wait for Poo-by to cop it!'

'Sasha, this is really risky …' started Ruby

'Nice try!' said Sasha cutting her off. 'Give me a bit of shush while I think up some nicknames for when you're bald.'

Sasha then gingerly sat on the bed and started calling out suggestions as they popped into her head.

'Baldy … Bald Eagle … Pumpkin Head … Badger, as in "bald as a badger" … Baldilocks — ooh I like that one! …'

Ruby shook her head as she lay down and began reading a Wonder Woman comic. But she was distracted moments later when Sasha started to scratch her head. *Uh oh.*

The scratching became more urgent, causing Sasha's hair to stick out at all angles, like a gigantic bird's nest. '*So* itchy!' she screamed.

This brought Miss Luxton rushing into the dorm, and she quickly inspected Sasha's scalp.

'Sweet Lord! That's the worst case of headlice I've ever seen. Follow me to the sick bay, Sasha … but not too close!'

An hour and a half later, Sasha re-entered the dorm wearing a towel wrapped around her head. 'If anyone says *anything*, they are *so* dead!' she snarled.

She took off the towel revealing that every single strand of her luxurious hair had been shaved off. This led to an explosion of laughter from all sections of the dorm, and Sasha fled out the door to hide in the bathroom.

Miranda walked over to Sasha's desk and picked up the drawing.

'I don't understand what hap—'

A shocked expression appeared on her face, and she slowly held up the drawing to show Ruby.

It was exactly the same as before, except where 'Ruby' had been written, it now said 'Sasha'.

'OMG!' said Miranda, jumping into her bed and hiding under the covers.

The next morning Ruby was awoken by a distinctive, high-pitched squeal.

She raced over to Fav's desk to find her looking at her laptop.

'Rubes, you are *not* going to believe it!'

'What?'

'Your cartoons have gone *viral!*'

'Is that good or bad?'

'Good! No, it's better than good, it's great!' said Fav. '#istandwithchirpy is the top trending hashtag on Twitter, and people are hanging out colourful scarves and sending their support from all over the world!'

Ruby was stunned. 'Are you sure?'

'Totally! The Wilderness Society, the World Wildlife Fund and a heap of other really cool organizations are getting behind us, and—'

'Fav, slow down!' pleaded Ruby. 'H-h-how is this happening?'

Fav quickly clicked on a link to the *Hetherington Herald*.

'Hey, we made the front page!' said Ruby.

The headline read: 'Theme Park threatens endangered bird!' and Ruby noticed all her cartoons were included with the article.

'And check out what Rosemary Arrow wrote,' said Fav. '"Twelve-year-old Ruby West's devastatingly clever cartoons portray the sad plight of the Gouldian Finch more effectively than any words can …"'

Ruby went bright red, as Fav grabbed her arm excitedly.

'And that's not all! You should hear what people are saying, like …' Fav quickly tapped the keyboard and instantly they were looking at some Twitter feeds.

'… "Ruby West and her friends are an inspiration to all of us!" And that's from an 89-year-old in San Francisco!'

'I still don't get it … how?'

'Rosemary's article and your drawings were picked up by all the national newspapers overnight. And everyone who read the articles loved your cartoons and started sending them all over the world. The UK, the United States, France, Russia, Germany, Japan, Africa, South America ...'

Ruby watched her friend tap the keyboard again, and the *Hetherington Herald* front page reappeared on the screen.

'Listen to this! Rosemary's article has just been updated: "With the whole world looking on, the Hetherington council is under extreme pressure to stop the theme park development, especially with a local election coming up next month.'"

Ruby cocked her head to one side and looked at Fav.

'Does that mean they *won't* be cutting down the trees?' she asked.

'It doesn't look like it!'

'Woohoo!'

Fav jumped out of her chair and gave Ruby a hug. They then performed an incredibly poorly co-ordinated victory dance that caused them both to crack up.

Ruby stopped laughing to catch her breath, and suddenly her eyes narrowed. She rushed over to an open window and stuck her head outside. There was a distant clanging sound coming from the direction of the forest.

'What is it?' asked Fav.

'I don't know,' answered Ruby. 'It sounds like drums being played by lots of non-musicians.'

Down below she spotted Mr Lemon striding past the boarding house towards the school. She looked back to where the strange noises were originating, and then back at the headmaster.

'Fav, get dressed, we have to go!'

'Where to?'

'The storeroom.'

'Urgh!' squeaked Fav.

'What's the matter?' asked Ruby.

'I just crawled over something soft and squishy!'

'Sounds like our baby possum is back,' said Ruby.

'Are you saying I just squished a cute little possum?'

'No … I'm saying you just squished a cute little possum's poo!'

The two friends soon made it to the vent above the headmaster's office and straight away Ruby could see Mr Lemon pacing back and forth below. The phone rang, and he rushed over to push the speaker button.

'Headmaster Lemon speaking.'

'Oliver, it's Michael Casterbridge …'

'Ah, Mr Mayor, just the person I wanted to speak to about our, um, little problem.'

'*Little* problem?' said Mayor Casterbridge. 'I've just had a call from the Environment Minister!'

'It's all going to be fine …'

'How?' thundered the mayor. 'You can't destroy the habitat of an endangered species!'

'That's true … but what if there *aren't* any endangered species in the habitat?'

'What do you mean?'

'I've just paid twenty people to go through the forest making as much noise as possible. There won't be any Golden Finchy thingies hanging around after they finish …'

Ruby's jaw tightened as the headmaster prattled on.

'… so, if you send your environmental inspectors around straight away, they'll confirm there are no birds in the forest, and then The Terminator can start terminating a few trees!'

'Um, Oliver, there's been a slight … complication …'

'Complication?'

'Yes, a court order to stop your project has just been lodged by a lawyer representing two local citizens …'

'Which local citizens?' yelled Mr Lemon.

'Their names are … Marley Chol and Faith Atkinson.'

Ruby did a small fist pump, while Mr Lemon scowled and shook his head.

'There's two teaching contracts I won't be renewing!' he roared.

'You'll probably get a call from their lawyer shortly, ordering you to halt the development.'

'Well … as I technically don't know about this court order, I can get the bulldozer to clear the land right now, yes?'

'Well, I suppose *technically* that's right …'

'Great. By the time that stupid lawyer calls me, I'll be able to say, "Oh what a shame, there's no forest left!"'

'Well I don't know … this could cause me a lot of problems …'

'Mayor Casterbridge, if my theme park goes ahead I will *double* the money Dave Sykes has already paid you.'

'Okay, do it!'

The headmaster hung up and quickly made another call.

'Lenny? I want The Terminator to start work right now … No, not in a few hours, *right now!*'

Mr Lemon slammed down the phone, leaned back in his chair and casually started picking his nose.

'Gross!' whispered Ruby, as she and Fav started scurrying back along the beam.

They climbed down through the trapdoor and onto the

shelving, then dashed out of the storeroom into the corridor.

'Fav, get to your laptop and tell *everyone* what's happening, and I'll try to stop the bulldozer.'

'How are you going to do that?'

Ruby looked at her friend and said, 'I don't have a clue.'

CHAPTER

17

Ruby ran as fast as she could towards the forest.

Her legs were aching and she was breathing heavily, yet she refused to slow down. Images of Chirpy kept flashing into her head, and she was determined not to let her tiny friend down.

Ruby darted through the hole in the picket fence and plunged into the sea of green trees and bushes. In her haste she brushed and scraped against the coarse vegetation, but barely noticed the blood that was streaming from her arms.

She tripped on a small root and fell down hard, scraping her knee in the process. Her head landed in a dirty puddle, and her face was completely covered in thick, dark mud. Without bothering to wipe off the muck, she leapt to her feet and kept running.

All of a sudden Ruby heard the almighty roar of an enormous engine starting up nearby. She sprinted towards the noise, and thirty seconds later she saw the bulldozer.

Her eyes bulged. It was much, much bigger than the yellow one the animals had destroyed. It had a large, polished black cabin and through the glass she could see Lenny in his blue singlet, wriggling around in his seat to make himself more comfortable. Suddenly the giant machine slipped into gear and slowly started moving towards a dense clump of trees.

Ruby didn't hesitate. She raced over and stood directly in front of the bulldozer. Despite being exhausted and covered in mud and blood, she lifted her head defiantly and stared directly at the driver.

Lenny's eyes widened and he quickly hit the brakes. The unexpected arrival of a fierce-looking twelve-year-old girl draped in sludge had completely caught him off guard. But he soon regained his composure, and a cruel smile appeared on his face.

He calmly put the bulldozer into reverse and then went forward on a different path, but Ruby ran sideways and once again blocked his way. She had no idea if the rumbling machine would stop and was terrified as the gigantic blade loomed in front of her.

A deafening screech pierced the air as Lenny slammed on the brakes and the oversized blade halted a metre from her

face. Ruby's heart was pounding and she was now bathed in sweat. The smell of diesel hung in the air as the roar of the engine signalled The Terminator was reversing.

Once again Lenny moved the bulldozer forward on a different angle and once again Ruby ran across to stand in front of it. This time the blade stopped so close to her that she could easily reach out and touch it.

Straight away Lenny reversed The Terminator and then swiftly moved forward on yet another trajectory. Despite being absolutely terrified, Ruby again rushed across to block its progress.

This scene was repeated over and over, and each time the blade stopped closer to where Ruby was standing.

Ruby noticed that Lenny was still smiling, and suddenly realized why. *He knows I'll get tired and have to stop.*

As the driver continued to play his callous game of cat and mouse, Ruby pushed herself to the point of exhaustion. She could barely lift her legs and was feeling lightheaded, but she clenched her fists and pushed through the pain. *I have to do this for Chirpy,* she told herself.

Just as she was about to collapse, Ruby thought she heard a sound. *Pitter patter, pitter patter, pitter patter.* It seemed to be getting closer but she wasn't sure, because in her dizzy state she had lost all sense of direction.

From out of nowhere, Mr Chol and Miss Atkinson appeared. They rushed over and stood on either side of Ruby, each reaching out and holding one of her hands.

'You've done an amazing job, Rubes!' said her art teacher, giving her hand a squeeze.

Ruby looked up at Lenny in The Terminator's cabin and noticed his evil smirk had disappeared.

The sound of more running feet echoed through the forest as another ten people arrived, and they also held hands and stood in front of the bulldozer. Lenny now looked confused.

Ruby thought she heard stampeding horses, but discovered it was stampeding people. At least a hundred of them! Among them she spotted Fav, Dougal, Andre and Rosemary Arrow, who all took their place in the line in front of the bulldozer. Incredibly, more and more people arrived to join the protest, and even though she was in pain, Ruby could not stop smiling.

Lenny looked totally deflated, and he hopped down from The Terminator's cabin and wiped his brow.

Ruby glanced to her left and saw the headmaster and a man dressed in red and black robes burst through the bushes. They ran over and stood in front of The Terminator, facing the long line of protesters.

'Who's the guy with Mr Lemon?' asked Ruby.

'Mayor Casterbridge,' said Miss Atkinson. 'A complete weasel.'

As soon as she heard the word 'weasel' Ruby had an idea for a cartoon. She imagined two weasels arguing, and one saying to the other, 'Don't try to *human* your way out of it!' She was starting to feel better.

Mr Chol folded his arms and glared at Mr Lemon and the mayor.

'We're not going anywhere until this development is officially cancelled,' Mr Chol announced. All the other protesters cheered in support.

'People, let's be sensible!' called out the mayor in a superior tone. 'This bulldozer driver is going about his lawful business, and you are all illegally trespassing.'

'And if you don't leave immediately, I'll call the police,' added Mr Lemon.

'We're here to stop the destruction of an endangered species' habitat,' said Miss Atkinson. The protesters responded with a chorus of whistles and applause.

The headmaster shook his head dismissively and waved his arms to signal the crowd to quieten down.

'You have been incorrectly informed, Faith,' he sneered. 'Look around — there's no endangered species here. I mean, where are these so-called Golden Finches?'

'It's *Gouldian* Finch!' yelled Fav.

'Whatevs!' said Mr Lemon. 'If you can't prove they live here, you will all have to leave … now!'

After a brief silence, Ruby started making some bird noises.

'Chirp, chirp. Chirp, chirp.'

Nothing.

The smirk on Mr Lemon's face grew wider.

'Chirp, chirp. Chirp, chirp.'

'As I was saying …' started the headmaster.

There was a sudden rainbow-coloured flash as Chirpy flew in and landed at Ruby's feet. He started walking back and forth and jumping up and down.

'Chirpy!'

All the protestors cheered their little mascot, who seemed to love the attention.

'Oh, come on!' complained Mr Lemon. 'It's only one bird!'

'Yes,' echoed the mayor, 'It's only one bird!'

'Who will vote out the mayor if this clearing goes ahead?' yelled Mr Chol.

More than five hundred hands shot up in the air. At this, the mayor turned pale.

'Lenny, you can go,' he quietly told the bulldozer driver.

'But, but …' stammered Mr Lemon.

'No buts,' hissed Mayor Casterbridge.

The mayor then puffed out his chest and walked over to stand with the line of protesters.

'I officially declare this land … saved!' he said enthusiastically.

His short speech was met with a stony silence, which was eventually broken by the voice of a feisty old nana who was leaning on a walking frame.

'I'm still not votin' for ya!' she yelled in the mayor's direction.

Mayor Casterbridge went bright red and everyone burst out laughing.

CHAPTER

18

A week before the end of the term, Fav sat down on Ruby's bed for a chat.

After a lengthy discussion about whether the meat served at dinner had been beef, lamb or chicken, they started talking about the pen.

'Do you miss it?' asked Fav.

'Not really. At first it felt like it was protecting me, and that was pretty cool. But in the end, it seemed to be pushing me to … to get whatever I wanted, whenever I wanted it.'

'So, you don't even think about it?'

'*Occasionally* I think it would be nice to change things with a quick doodle. Ending global warming would be nice, and I'd love to …'

She stopped as she felt a lump forming in her throat.

'Love to what?' asked Fav.

'… bring my dad back.'

Fav reached out and touched Ruby's shoulder. 'I totally get that.'

'But … using the pen doesn't really solve anything. It only papers over the cracks, or ends up making things worse …'

Ruby and Fav's conversation was suddenly interrupted by Sasha. Her beautiful hair had just started to grow back, and most of the swelling from the bee attack had disappeared.

'Um, Ruby, if, just say, I give you the pen, will you use it to get back at me?'

'I promise not to use it on you … or anyone.'

Sasha glanced at the pen then looked back at Ruby.

'A promise is a promise, right?'

Ruby nodded and Sasha tentatively handed her the pen.

Ruby wasn't sure what to expect, but as the pen touched her hand she felt … nothing at all. No surge of warm energy. No desire to crush anyone who stood in her way. Nothing.

A smile of relief broke out on Ruby's face. Sasha started to walk off, but stopped and turned around.

'Hey, that thing you both did to save that bird was um … pretty awesome.'

Ruby and Fav were stunned and exchanged a quick glance.

'Um … thanks,' said Fav.

'Yeah, thanks,' said Ruby.

'You know, you two aren't too bad,' said Sasha. 'I just wish …'

'Wish what?' asked Fav.

'That you'd both do something to fix your hair!'

Ruby and Fav burst out laughing, and then Sasha joined in.

'No, I'm serious,' said Sasha. 'You could both look *so* good! Let me do your hair for the end-of-term Parents' Day — I promise you won't regret it.'

Ruby looked at Fav and they both shrugged their shoulders.

'We'll think about it,' said Fav.

'That's all I ask,' said Sasha before walking back to her desk.

Ruby sighed as she packed the last of her comic books into her bag.

It was end-of-term Parents' Day and she was excited about seeing her mum, but also sad that it was her last day at Hetherington Hall.

Fav had once told her that bees have a memory span of only two and a half seconds, and Ruby figured that would make saying goodbye a lot easier. She had drawn a cartoon featuring two bees, with one saying, 'Farewell to the best friend I've ever had … hey, who are you?'

And the other bee replies, 'I don't know.'

Ruby's relationship with her mum had begun to thaw after Adelaide had sent her an email a few weeks ago.

Hey Rubes,

Just read in the paper about what you and your friends are doing to save Chirpy and the beautiful forest — your drawings were incredibly powerful. So proud of you, and your dad would be too!

Lots of love, Mum xx

It had been a special message because Adelaide *had* mentioned her father and *hadn't* mentioned Dodgy Dave.

Before zipping up her bags, Ruby checked her cupboard one last time to make sure she hadn't left anything behind.

'Hey, Rubes!'

A smile broke out on her face and she spun around.

'Mum!'

Straight away she could see a difference in her mother's eyes. *The sparkle is back!*

Ruby gave her a hug, and then Adelaide took a step back to inspect her daughter.

'I absolutely love your hair,' she said.

'I told you so!' called out Sasha from the other side of the dorm. Ruby rolled her eyes.

'Thanks, Mum! I'll be hearing about that for the rest of the day.'

Adelaide sat down on the bed, and Ruby tried to steer the conversation away from her new 'look'.

'So, how are you?' she asked Adelaide.

'Pretty good. I've … um … broken up with Dave.'

'Fantastic! I mean, sorry to hear that.'

Adelaide smiled.

'You never liked him …'

'He wasn't *that* bad,' said Ruby.

'No … he was worse!' said Adelaide with a grin. 'And don't worry, no more boyfriends for me for quite a while.'

'Good. Have you moved out?'

'Yep, I'm renting a little two-bedroom flat. It's tiny, but it's clean and neat, and I hope you're going to like it.'

'Cool, Mum, but how can …'

'… I afford it? Your mother's got a job! I'm helping out the curator at the local gallery. Only three days a week, but …'

'Mum, that's unreal! I'm so proud of you.'

Adelaide sighed and looked around the room. 'I'm just sorry I can't afford to keep you here.'

'That's okay.'

Adelaide sighed again. 'Rubes, sometimes I wish someone could write both of us a happy ending.'

Ruby glanced over at the old, battered pen on her desk.

'Mum, supposing there *was* someone who could write us a happy ending ...' Ruby slowly walked over, picked up the pen, then put it into her alligator pencil case before zipping it up tight. '... I wouldn't want them to. I'd much rather we sort it out ourselves.'

Adelaide nodded.

'There's so much I want to talk to you about when we get home, Rubes,' she said. 'About how sorry I am for not being there for you, and about how much I miss your dad.'

'I miss him too. That's why we need to look out for each other.'

Ruby moved forward and gave her mum a hug. A real hug. A hug full of love and warmth. She closed her eyes and smiled.

A bell went off in the background, and Ruby slowly pulled back from her mum to check her watch.

'Time for final assembly.'

A hum of excitement hung in the air as the parents and students took their seats inside the large hall.

Ruby and Adelaide sat next to Fav and her parents. Fav's mum was short, incredibly enthusiastic and wore round glasses and a friendly smile. *Now I know what Fav will look like in twenty-five years*, thought Ruby.

'You girls look stunning with your hair like that,' said Mrs Sharma.

'I told you so,' said Sasha, who was just sitting down with her parents in the row in front of them. Ruby and Fav rolled their eyes, then listened in as Mrs Sword started criticizing everything and everybody around her.

'How uncomfortable are these chairs? They should make that groundsman shave off those awful sideburns. Did you notice Miss Vermin was wearing plastic earrings? Plastic!'

Ruby turned to her mum and they both shook their heads and had a quiet giggle.

She looked across to her left and spotted Andre sitting next to Anne-Marie and a man she assumed was Andre's father. She waved and all three of them waved back enthusiastically.

Dougal was sitting in the same row, and he pulled a funny face and gave Ruby a thumbs-up. She immediately pulled a funny face of her own and smiled back at him. She sighed then turned to Fav and said, 'I'm going to miss you all *so* much next term!'

'Promise you'll email me every single day, Rubes.'

'I promise, cross my heart ...'

A chorus of 'shhhh' from all around the old hall made Ruby look towards the stage. She was surprised to see Mr Chol striding towards the lectern, with the other teachers seated behind him.

'Psst Fav, where's Mr Lemon?' asked Ruby. Fav shrugged her shoulders as Mr Chol started to speak.

'Distinguished guests, ladies and gentleman and of course our wonderful students ... welcome! My name is Marley Chol, and the school board has asked me to be Hetherington Hall's acting headmaster while Mr Lemon is assisting the police with their enquiries.'

'OMG!' said Ruby as everyone rose to their feet and clapped. The acting headmaster smiled appreciatively and waited for the audience to sit down before continuing.

'We've seen many changes this term, both at the school and in our local community. The town even has a new mayor, who is the mother of one of our students, so congratulations to Connie Rundle. And it's great to hear that her son Jeremy has made an excellent recovery from chicken pox and will be back at school next term.' Ruby looked at the floor, feeling relieved and embarrassed at the same time.

'Now I'd like to call on Miss Atkinson to share some very special news,' said Mr Chol.

Miss Atkinson rose from her seat with a smile, as the audience clapped supportively.

'Yes, it is *very* special news,' she said from the lectern. 'A brand-new *full* scholarship has been kindly donated by the Amano family. This scholarship is for students with artistic talent and integrity, and it is my great privilege to announce the first ever recipient … Ruby West!'

Ruby's jaw dropped and her heart started pounding wildly. She felt as if her brain was about to explode, but managed to compose herself enough to look over and mouth 'thank you' to Mr and Mrs Amano. Adelaide started sobbing joyfully and gave Ruby a hug.

As everyone stood up and applauded, tears welled in Ruby's eyes. 'I really hope this isn't a dream,' she whispered to her mum.

As the clapping started to die down, Ruby overheard Mrs Sword talking to Sasha.

'I saw that girl's dreadful drawings in the school magazine, and they weren't even funny!'

'Mum, please!' snapped Sasha. 'Ruby is a … pretty good artist.'

Ruby turned to Fav and they both raised their eyebrows

before giving each other a quick squeeze.

'Guess we'll be seeing each other next term after all,' said Fav.

'So do I still have to email you every day?' joked Ruby

'A promise is a promise!' said Fav, and they both burst out laughing.

CHAPTER

19

The sun shone brightly as powerful, foam-crested waves crashed over the sleek dark rocks on the beach below.

'I never thought I'd be able to come back here,' said Adelaide, as they stared out over the spot where Bertie had died.

'Me either,' said Ruby. 'But we need to let go of the past, so we can move on.'

Adelaide took a deep breath and reached into her pocket.

She pulled out a small object and flung it as far as she could into the ocean. It made a jangling sound as it sped through the air before plopping noiselessly into the sea.

'What was that?' asked Ruby.

'The keys to Dodgy Dave's Porsche!'

Ruby laughed out loud.

'The Porsche you were never allowed to drive?'

'Yep! I thought your father would find that pretty funny, too.'

Adelaide reached into her pocket again, then threw something else into the water.

'And what was that?' asked Ruby.

'Dave's spare set!'

'Mum! You are terrible … but you're right, Dad would love this.'

Ruby slid her hand into her pocket, and slowly retrieved the pen.

She gave it a quick kiss and whispered, 'Thank you.' She then launched the pen with all her might, and it hurtled end over end through the air, before being swallowed by the deep blue water.

'What was that?' asked Adelaide.

'Something I don't need any more.'

Ruby turned and hugged her mum as she gazed out to sea.

Goodbye Dad, I love you.

Epilogue

The next day in a town called Dukescliff …

Xander's pursuers were closing on him as he sped through the market's entrance and began weaving between the laid-back locals.

'Give up, Beast!' yelled Jeff.

'Yeah — you're only making things worse!' roared Tony.

Suddenly the temperature plunged and Xander could not see anything. It was as if someone had turned off the sun. The thick mist had made it to shore, instantly enveloping the entire seaside marketplace.

Xander dropped to his knees. Just before losing visibility, he had spotted a line of portable toilets to his left and had begun crawling in that direction, so he could hide around the back of them. But the sound of Bruise Brothers' voices made him stop in his tracks.

'Where'd he go?' asked Tony.

'Dunno — he was right here,' replied Jeff.

'Okay, let's check from here up to the end of the row. Even though we can't see him, he can't be far away.'

Xander let out a deep sigh and resumed crawling.

Unfortunately he slightly misjudged the distance, and ended up locating the toilets with his head. 'Ouch!'

Ignoring the pain, Xander felt his way around the back and lay down on his stomach. He took some deep breaths to get as much air back into his lungs as possible. Xander knew he had to escape before the cover of the fog disappeared. As he stood up, his left hand pressed against something on the ground. It was money — notes and coins.

The mist was too thick for Xander to see how much cash was there, but he gratefully stuffed it into his pocket.

He set off waving his hands in front of him so that he would detect any obstacles before colliding into them. Lots of people had turned on their phones' torches, so he carefully avoided any luminous circles of light that permeated the grey mass surrounding him. The fog's density began to lessen, which helped him gain his bearings.

The exit was now fairly close but just as Xander was about to slip away, a golden flash of light caught his attention.

Then another golden flash erupted — this one was even bigger.

It seemed to come from the market stall at the end of the row.

Despite the risk, Xander decided to sneak over and find out what was going on.

He squinted at the sign above the stall. It looked like it said 'Second Hand Treasures' but he couldn't be completely sure. He could vaguely make out the unusual assortment of objects on the unsteady trestle table — antique lamps, a variety of colourful crystals and … a pen.

Even in the poor light Xander could tell it was a very old pen. It was scratched and battered but had striking gold writing on the side.

Xander didn't know why, but he felt drawn to it. His hand trembled as he reached out to pick it up and …

Zap! A warm surge of power flowed from the pen directly into Xander's fingers, then up his arm before spreading throughout his entire body.

In an instant he felt safe, like he was wearing a protective layer of armour.

'Nothing can harm me,' he whispered.

He smiled as he stared at the pen, then tried to make sense of the strange writing on its side.

'*Manibus futuri.*'

'That's Latin,' said a deep voice from the other side of the table.

Xander's head jerked up to see an odd-looking old man wearing a purple robe covered in yellow moons and stars, with a matching circular hat. The skin on his face looked like well-worn leather and his eyes sparkled with mischief.

'S-s-sorry?' replied Xander.

'The writing on the pen — it's Latin,' said the man.

'Latin?'

'An ancient language.'

Xander re-examined the words.

'Man-i-bus fu-tur-i,' he said.

'It means, "The future is in your hands",' explained the elderly man. 'If you're interested in buying it, it's …'

He put his hand on his chin and looked Xander up and down, before giving a small nod. '… fifteen dollars and forty cents.'

Xander gently replaced the pen on the table. 'Um, no thanks,' he said. 'I don't have any money.'

'That's a pity,' said the man.

Xander dejectedly shoved his hand into his pocket and was instantly reminded of his discovery behind the portable toilets.

'Wait! I *do* have some money!'

He started pulling the cash out of his pocket and counting it on the trestle table.

'There's ten dollars, and, um, hang on, there's another five … and twenty cents, and another ten, um and here's five more — how much is that?'

'That's fifteen dollars and thirty-five cents,' said the man. 'You're five cents short.'

Xander's face dropped.

'Are you sure there's no more money in your pocket?' asked the man.

Xander delved back into his pocket and fished around again.

'No … wait a sec!'

With a beaming smile Xander pulled out another five-cent piece. 'Fifteen dollars forty exactly!' he said.

'Excellent. Now it's an ink pen, so you'll need some ink …'

Xander folded his arms and glared at the purple-robed salesman.

'Don't worry — the ink is included in the price.'

Xander let out a small sigh as the man handed him an ornate bottle filled with a dark liquid.

'Thanks!'

He quickly unzipped his school bag and put the pen and bottle of ink inside.

'No, thank *you*,' said the mysterious man.

Book 2

Coming soon!